To the best Momma Gay in the whole world!

Signature

Flaggers Bridge

Sonya Carlan

*This book is dedicated to my loving sister Shelly
Ladd who always believed in me when I didn't
even believe in myself.*

TATE PUBLISHING
AND **ENTERPRISES**, LLC

Published by Tate Publishing & Enterprises, LLC
127 E. Trade Center Terrace | Mustang, Oklahoma 73064 USA
1.888.361.9473 | www.tatepublishing.com

Tate Publishing is committed to excellence in the publishing industry. The company reflects the philosophy established by the founders, based on Psalm 68:11,
"The Lord gave the word and great was the company of those who published it."

Published in the United States of America

ISBN: 978-1-63367-079-2
1. Fiction / Christian / General
2. Fiction / Coming Of Age
14.05.28

Chapter 1

The wind was cruelly biting into the back of her neck. The days had only been into the high 20s for the last three weeks which meant the nights were arctic in the single digits. Standing in the dark out on this bridge was definitely colder than she could've ever imagined. The wind chill factor must be fifteen below. Her face was beginning to feel like the bones were being compressed and would break any minute. How could it be so cold so far south? She started to turn the collar of her fleece jacket up over her nose but she realized how silly that idea was.

Here she was standing in the middle of the night, a freezing cold hypothermic night, on the north bound side of Flaggers Bridge trying to build up her nerve to fling herself over the side and suddenly she's concerned with keeping warm. It almost made her giggle. Shaking her head slowly she reached up and rubbed both palms across her numbing face.

Why was she still just standing here like an idiot? What could possibly matter enough now that didn't matter an hour ago? It must be something, she thought, because an hour ago she was positive that this was her only option. It was her only chance for peace. Now she was hesitating. Why? She had to just do it; she had to just clear her mind and do it. It would be over soon. It would be quick. If the fall didn't kill her, the cold water would, shutting her body down in seconds. She had researched this before. The last thing she wanted was to throw herself off of a bridge and survive. Life was bad enough already; she couldn't bear the thought of 'living' on in a wheelchair or vegetating in a semi-conscious state for the rest of her years.

Sucking in a sharp stinging breath, she hardened her resolve and hiked up her leg to climb the side of the iron railing when she saw lights coming out of the darkness and approaching the bridge in the south bound lane. Panic flooded her. Quick, she had to be quick before someone stopped her.

She managed to get her right leg up onto the railing as she heard the vehicle slowing down. She grabbed the cold iron attempting to hoist her left leg upward as well, but, suddenly she seemed hung. Oh, God, this cannot be happening to me, she thought. I've got to hurry.

The frenzy to get up the railing had taken over and she was in full flight mode. The only problem was that she couldn't move. Something had her nailed in place. She couldn't go further up the railing and it seemed she couldn't even come down. The frightened girl tried to pull free of whatever held her captive but it was no use.

The oncoming car had stopped and she could hear a voice calling out in the darkness.

"Hello? Ma'am are you ok?" the man's voice bellowed over the brutal wind. He was walking across the lane towards this girl who seemed to be glued like a spider to the side of the bridge. She could see his

2

silhouette as it blocked out the light from the car headlights.

The man reached her side of the bridge, cautiously at first, but then he picked up the pace when it became obvious to him that this young girl was attempting to take her life. Nobody would be out in this weather just to pull a stunt that could cost them an arm and leg. Or more.

"Honey, I don't know what's wrong but this is NOT the answer. My name is Curtis and I'm the pastor over at Dunlevy Baptist Church, over in Bramwell. You heard of it?"

She didn't answer, only clung to the side of the rail shivering uncontrollably. She had been out in this cold for too long and it was beginning to cause her to hurt all over. She wanted to die more than ever now only she wasn't sure if it was from the cold or embarrassment.

"Listen, it seems that you're pants are snagged on this metal bar. That means you aren't going any further up. I would love to help you down, get you out of this cold and maybe have a talk. Please let me help you. Freezing to death on the side of this bridge would be an awful way to die."

She started to cry but even her tears were freezing to her face. She felt utterly hopeless. She angled her head a bit where she could see the man talking to her. He was an older man. She couldn't see much in the dark but she could tell by his shape he was no spring chicken.

This poor man was standing out in subzero temperatures trying to help her and she was being difficult. She didn't want to come down but she wasn't going to be able to go up. She could either relent or carry the burden of this old preacher man freezing to death trying to talk her off a ledge. She made eye contact through the blurry light of the headlight glow.

"My...my name is Addy. Can you help me down please?" she stuttered.

3

The man exhaled as if he had been holding his breath forever. He never thought in a million years that he would be driving home from a late night men's bible study to find a young girl in need of rescue on the Flaggers Bridge. He guessed it was a good thing that God caused her to be stuck to the side because at his age he wasn't able to carry out any physical heroics to save anyone. Of course he was aware that God had left this girl here for him to find. He felt it in his spirit. He wasn't sure what her story was or what his part in it would be but he had to see how it was going to play out. It was his duty as a Christian to help hurting souls and it seemed that this young girl was hurting enough for several people.

Curtis made the few more steps that would take him to the railing and began to pull at the fabric caught on the bridge. The second hard tug pulled the material away with only a small rip and suddenly he had his hand on the girl's wrist. He would not be letting her go until she was safely in his car.

Addy's body was screaming in pain from the cold and her hands were as numb as her face. The man eased her off the rail and guided her to his car. Once he had her in the vehicle, the heat hit her face and she cried as the feeling came back into her body. She didn't realize how warming up could be so terribly painful.

Curtis climbed into the driver's side of his Bonneville and turned on the interior light. This young girl was pitiful. Her reddish brown hair was medium length and looked as though someone had painstakingly tied it into a tangled mass of knots. It was probably the wind whipping it around that caused the mess of hair, he thought. She wasn't very old, was reed thin, and carried a look of pain in her eyes that struck Curtis to the core. Her black fleece jacket shook with the sobs she unleashed. At the ripe old age of 63, Curtis had been a pastor for most of his life but for some reason he never was too comfortable with crying children.

4

He and his wife had never had any children of their own. It wasn't on purpose, just happened that way. His wife, Helen, filled the void with the children in the church. No matter how many different churches over the years, you could always count on there being kids who needed good strong authority figures to show them love. Helen was that kind of person. She believed no kid should go unloved. Now with this lost girl in his car, he wasn't sure what he should do with her.

Helen would know.

Helen always knew what to do with troubled kids. He would take her home and turn her over to Helen.

Chapter 2

By the time they reached the pastor's house, Addy had stopped crying and was simply staring out into the night like a zombie. It was like an out of body experience. She was being propelled along by an unseen force and despair had settled in so deep that she didn't even care. She would just go through the motions until her broken heart simply stopped beating. It had to happen soon because there was no way any human being could feel the pain she was feeling and live through it. She would just go with the flow until that final day came when she could close her eyes forever. That was her plan.

Helen Campbell just happened to be lying in bed wide awake when she saw her husband's headlights pull in the drive. Thank God, she thought. On nights like this she always harbored a tiny bit of worry when he was running late. She trusted in the Lord and had faith but Helen knew that bad things happen to good people sometimes and we may never know the reason why. A small part of her was always on the lookout for that bit of fate. She was 59 years old and had been married to the love of her life for over 40 years.

She and Curtis had been together when they were foolish teenagers who thought life was a breeze when you grow up. They were together when God called Curtis to preach and he didn't have anyone to preach to. The years that they didn't have two nickels to rub together had only brought them closer. Now, she couldn't imagine her life without him although it was inevitable unless she went first. Sometimes she hoped it would be her to go first but the thought of leaving Curtis alone broke her heart. She could only hope that God called them home together. If not, they would handle it the best way they could.

It took her husband much longer than normal to get into the house and out of concern Helen got out of bed and pulled her faded yellow robe over her nightgown to check on him. She headed out of the bedroom and down the stairs on bare feet. When she reached the bottom, the front door eased open and Curtis was leading a young girl by the elbow into their home.

This child looked terrible. Whatever had transpired tonight was not good. It didn't take a genius to see that. Standing there holding onto the poor girl made Helen see how the years had changed her once strong and virile husband.

Curtis was never extremely tall for a man but he did stand around five foot eleven and weigh in around one-ninety. He caught many of the girls' eyes back in his day. Helen had been proud that he had chosen her when he could have had his pick.

Now his usually straight frame looked somewhat bent and haggard. The wrinkles around his eyes and mouth told of the many nights he stayed on his knees crying out to God for a sick church member or for the salvation of a loved one. His soft brown eyes had seen so many miracles but also so much pain. When you preach the word, it's never as easy as it looks on the outside. Curtis'

7

thinning brown hair had turned salt and pepper many years ago but to Helen, he was still her hero.

He looked up to see his wife standing on the stairs in her robe looking down on him with concern. He nodded his head for her to follow them as he led the distressed girl into the den and sat her down on the sofa. No sign of life came from the girl. If her eyes had been closed Helen would have been sure she was comatose.

"Well, who do we have here?" Helen asked softly. The silence was so palpable that it felt as if raising your voice would cause this girl to shatter into a million pieces.

"This is Addy, honey. She and I met on Flaggers Bridge tonight. She's a bit cold so I thought we could find her some warm pajamas and maybe a hot bite to eat, get to know each other better."

Curtis smiled while talking but Helen could see the dark shadows of worry under his eyes. Whatever had brought this girl to him was serious.

"I think that sounds like a great idea. I was just thinking of getting up and having a midnight snack myself when you both arrived. It's very nice to meet you Addy. I'm Helen."

Helen extended her hand but the girl just continued to sit staring into space. It was as if her soul had left her body and she was a shell of what she once was. Helen motioned for Curtis to move across the room with her.

"Good Lord what happened to this child? What was she doing on the bridge at this time of night? Where are her parents?"

With every question Helen seemed to be more alarmed. Curtis reached for his wife's hand and told her the brief story of how he found Addy hung on the side of the bridge attempting to throw herself over. He also told his wife that the only information he had gotten so far was her first name and a simple request for him to help her down. In a flash of a moment standing on that bridge Curtis had felt the Holy Spirit tell him to help this girl.

8

He wasn't sure how, just that he had been called to do it. The real test seemed to be the 'how' of the situation.

First things first, they had to get her talking.

Chapter 3

As soft and loving as Helen Campbell was, she was still the wife of a pastor and that came with a requirement of a sturdy backbone. You had to know when to coddle someone and when to give tough love. She was a good reader of people. Discernment was one of her gifts and she was almost always on the mark.

She had excused herself from the den to go into the kitchen for food. She had known that Curtis would not be home until late because of the bible study so dinner leftovers were scarce. She opened up a can of chicken noodle soup and poured it into a pot on the stove. While the soup heated, she quickly put together a cheese sandwich on white bread. With both items on a tray and a glass of iced tea she made her way back to the den. Never having any children of their own, the Campbell home was neat and tidy with lovingly worn furniture, brightly colored afghans draped over the sofa and chairs, as well as knitted doilies adorning the end tables. It was a place that you could feel safe.

Helen sat the tray down on the coffee table in front of Addy and turned to her husband.

"Could you give me and Addy a moment alone dear? Please go gather some clean linen for the guest room while we talk."

She beamed a bright smile on her husband as if it was tea time for the girls and she was having the best of days. Trusting his wife's judgment, he nodded and excused himself from the room.

Lord let me do your will and not my own, Helen thought as she sat down on the sofa beside the girl. She placed her hand over Addy's lifeless arm and began to talk softly.

"Sweetie, I understand that whatever happened to you feels bad enough that you want to give up on life right now but that is just not an option. No one's life is easy and there are many of us that go through terribly traumatic things but we must go on. Now Curtis and I are here to help you no matter what you're going through but you have to communicate with us. I do not allow strong, beautiful young women like you to sit in my home and just give up. So I don't care how you start it or what you want to talk about but you ARE going to talk to me young lady."

With that being said, Helen continued to look at Addy with kindness and waited. It was almost five whole minutes of silence before the girl began to cry softly.

"Addy McMullen. That's my name ma'am. My full name is Adelicia Renee McMullen and I used to live on Marchess Street in Vigoss County."

The tears came on hard and Helen wrapped her arms around the child while she sobbed uncontrollably. This was a beginning. She had broken through.

When Curtis returned to the den he could hear the muffled weeping before he reached the doorway. His wife was holding Addy and smoothing down her hair

11

while she slowly cried it all out. Helen looked up and smiled faintly at him letting him know she had gotten somewhere with the girl. He knew she would. Helen had that way with people. She always had.

The first time he ever saw Helen she was a little over sixteen years old and she seemed to be holding court in the parking lot of the town theater. She had four or five other girls around her who were hanging on every word she said. Her long honey colored hair was neatly braided down the center of her back and she held her school books in her crossed arms as she leaned against a gold Pontiac GTO.

Curtis was four years her senior at twenty and was already working for a living. He never had any problem getting dates. He was actually somewhat of a ladies man but none of them ever really kept his interest for long. The spark faded too quickly.

He couldn't take his eyes off the vibrant girl bobbing her head as she talked and laughed; she was simply captivating. He couldn't explain it but he just had to know her. His buddy Cal had pulled up in the spot beside him and was getting out of the car when Curtis decided to be spontaneous.

That day when he introduced himself to the pretty little girl named Helen was the best day of his life. He just knew she was 'the one' and when God came knocking on his heart's door, it was flung wide open. He knew why Helen was 'the one;' because God knew that nobody else would love him the way he had to be loved to make it through all the trials of being a pastor. She was his rock and he was never sorry that he made her his wife.

Looking at her now with a little gray in her honey colored hair and the laugh lines around her eyes, he was still amazed. She had somehow gotten this girl to open up to her. He cleared his throat to be polite and both females looked his way.

"The guest room is ready dear."

Curtis crossed the room to take a seat in a chair opposite the sofa. He had to move several crocheted throw pillows to be able to sit down. He watched as Addy took a few bites of her sandwich and soup while Helen remained at her side, stroking her back in a motherly fashion. The patience that the couple showed had been cultivated over many years of dealing with people who came to them for everything from saving their life to just lending a sympathetic ear to their problems.

"I'm going to go up and find you something warm and comfortable to sleep in and I'll be right back dear," Helen whispered as she patted Addy's leg. The girl nodded as she placed her glass of tea on the tray in front of her.

When Helen had gone from the room, Addy looked up at Pastor Curtis. He had been flipping through a fishing magazine he pulled out of a basket beside the chair. It was close to 2:00 a.m. and Addy knew these people had to be exhausted. She couldn't recall how long it had been since someone had shown her this type of kindness; or if anyone ever had at all.

In a husky cracked voice she said, "Thank you sir. Thank you for caring about me enough to pull me off that bridge like you did. Most people would have driven by and pretended not to see." She shrugged her shoulders slightly and continued, "People don't usually like to get drug into other people's problems, you know?"

She kept breaking eye contact as if she were ashamed to hold his gaze. She would look down at her scarred hands. She had a terrible nervous habit of picking at the skin around her cuticles. She had made a mess of her fingers over time and now they were badly scarred. It seemed she did it instinctively and without realizing it.

Curtis thought a moment before speaking. He templed his fingers on his lips for just long enough to gather his thoughts.

"I should be the one thanking you Addy."

13

This comment made the girl look up with a quizzical brow, waiting for him to explain what he meant. When he did not explain further she finally asked, "Why? I'm the one who ruined your night."

"Ruined my night? You didn't ruin anything Addy. Shoot, I get to tell my friends that I singlehandedly rescued a young girl from falling off a bridge! When you're my age, that kind of story earns bragging rights at the next men's bible study."

A small smile started across her face as she said, "I'm glad I could be of service sir."

Curtis winked at the girl as Helen returned from her errand of locating a suitable set of pajamas for Addy to wear. Helen asked Addy to follow her upstairs and Curtis bid goodnight to the two of them. Watching them head up, he thought 'What in the world are we doing?'

There had been many times over the years when he had counseled people, with and without Helen, but something seemed so different about this girl. He had never actually brought someone home with him in this way. Being a lead pastor had also kept him on the official end of counseling sessions. There's a hierarchy even in religion and one thing you learn early on is that the lead pastor cannot be superman and solve everyone's issues even if he wants to. You have to delegate!

So, many years of delegating had brought him to the place where he sent people to the various leaders in his congregation. He had a lady, who was over women's ministries, a deacon for men's ministries, and a youth leader. He very rarely handled any one-on-one counseling anymore and was beginning to feel that he may not be up to snuff.

What if this young lady turned out to have issues he or Helen was not equipped to handle? Should he call someone else and turn her over to them in the morning?

Suddenly he felt a stirring of the spirit and he could hear these words, 'If I had wanted her to be found by

14

someone else, I would have arranged for someone else to be driving by.' He felt instantly ashamed of himself for attempting to pass the buck. God never positions you for anything you are not equipped to handle, whether you think so or not. Curtis knew that but he was human and was entitled to a little doubt every now and again.

Chapter 4

Curtis waited quietly downstairs for Helen to return. He knew that once she got Addy tucked into bed she would be back to discuss this whole situation. She came down the stairs about fifteen minutes later. She looked tired and squinty-eyed. Helen plopped down hard on the sofa, leaned back and closed her eyes.

"Well, I got her full name and an idea of where she's from. She came from Vigoss; must have walked from town to the Flaggers. She says she used to live on Marchess Street. I'm not sure what 'used to' means but her last name is McMullen. You need to call Phil over at the station when it gets a decent hour; see if he's got any runaways or missing persons that match her name or description. No need doing it tonight. It's obvious that whatever drove her out there to end it all needs to be talked about in the light of day. She needed food and sleep, just like we do. So now that you're through being a defender of the damsel in distress, can we get some shut eye before dawn?"

Helen smiled at Curtis sweetly.

"Yes my love. You head on up. I'm going to throw a pillow here on the couch and keep my ear out for anything crazy. We don't need her trying to sneak out and finish the job while we sleep."

Curtis was pulling his shoes off and sliding them under the coffee table. His wife smiled and walked over to kiss him on the cheek.

"You're a good man Curt Campbell. See you in the morning."

Curtis cracked his eyes open to the sound of his wife in the kitchen. He could smell sausage frying and coffee brewing. He sat up stiffly and stretched. The few hours of sleep he had gotten were deep but uncomfortable. He had slept in his clothes just in case he had to get up for an emergency. His dreams cycled back to the cold winter wind howling and Addy on the bridge; except in his dreams he was too late. He would watch in horror as she leapt over the side. He could hear the screaming fading away as she dropped lower and lower to the water. Was it her screams or his own he heard ringing in his ears?

He scrubbed his fists in his eyes then stood up to make his way into the kitchen. Helen was flitting from counter to stove as swift as a hummingbird. Her short and smartly styled hair cut, belying her true age, looked chic as usual. You could not tell that his wife had only the same four hours sleep that he had enjoyed. She always looked ready for the day. Of course her dreams were probably not filled with visions of suicide like his were. He did not feel like sharing that particular bit of information with her. Talking about it made him remember it and remembering the dreams made him feel scared and helpless.

"Where's Addy? She up yet?" He looked at his watch as he asked the question. Twelve minutes after eight -- wow, he had not realized it was that late. Helen handed him a cup of coffee and he sat down at the table.

17

"I haven't seen her yet. I went up to make sure she was okay and she was sleeping like a log. I figure sleep is good for her. I'll wake her up when it's time to eat."

Curtis reached over and grabbed the phone off the bar. It was time to call his friend Phil over at the sheriff's department. He was the sheriff of Polton County which was where Curtis and Helen lived; more specifically the city of Bramwell, Georgia. According to what Addy told Helen last night, she was from the neighboring county of Despin, city of Vigoss. That was only about ten minutes from the Flaggers Bridge where he found her.

Phil may not have any direct information on her but he would know who to call for any possible leads. He dialed the number and the line began to ring.

"Polton County Sheriff's Department. How may I direct your call?" said the voice on the other end of the line.

"Pastor Curt Campbell to speak with Sheriff Anderson please."

"One moment sir," the polite lady deputy responded.

There was a brief pause as his call was transferred and quickly answered by the sheriff.

"Curt old man! How's the weather at your house?"

That was their greeting every time they talked for the last twenty years of their friendship. Their houses were two miles apart so whatever the weather at Curt's house was, the weather at Phil's house must be the same. A redundant question but it was a man thing. Of course 'the weather' that Phil was asking about was not the actual outdoor climate. It was a euphemism for 'what's your day like so far'. Curt knew this so he responded in like fashion.

"It's downright stormy old friend. I need your professional help. You got any missing persons reports for a young girl by the name of Addy McMullen? She's about five foot five, around 115 pounds, reddish hair. Sound familiar?"

18

"Hmmm...can't say I do old buddy. Let me look in the out-of-town box. We're all the time getting information from other stations. If I turn anything up I'll give you a call. What's your interest in this girl? Is she a member of your congregation?"

"No, just looking into something for a friend. Hey I appreciate it man. I'll talk to you soon."

The men said their goodbyes and hung up.

"No luck?" Helen asked.

Curtis shook his head no. He might take a ride later on and see if he could locate this Marchess Street over in Vigoss.

Chapter 5

The sun shining through the window by the bed slowly woke Addy. Her body ached all over like she had been drug behind a large semi-truck all night. It all seemed foggy like a drug induced dream. Why did her leg burn like it was cut?

She struggled to open her swollen eyes as they slowly focused on pale yellow wallpaper covered with tiny lilies. Where was she? Panic started to rise up in her throat. Suddenly it all flooded back to her. She was at the home of the man who saved her life.

Wow, the impact of what she had done hit her like a ten ton weight and she raised her hand to her head. How do you screw up suicide? She guessed she could write a book on it now since she was obviously an expert. She felt like an idiot. What must these people think of her? They had been so kind last night. She didn't deserve their kindness. If they knew what kind of person she was, they wouldn't have saved her.

She sat up on the side of the bed and cradled her head in her hands. The grief was crushing. A lonely tear escaped her eye as it all came rushing back, just like it did every morning of her life. She slowly tipped over to lie on her side. She stared through the little window that was filling the room with light.

Did anyone else feel like she did? She hoped not. She didn't want to feel this way either. Closing her eyes again, she prayed sleep would take her again but it wouldn't. Only the memories were swirling around behind her closed lids.

Being the only daughter of an upper-middle-class family had its perks. They weren't freaks. They had their problems like most families but as a whole, it was good. Nobody could argue that fact, at least not in the early years.

Addy spent her high school years playing soccer, softball, participating in the FFA and Decca clubs. She took swimming lessons and karate, piano and guitar. If she wanted to do it, her parents made it happen. They weren't rich but they believed in providing a better life for their daughter than they had been afforded. The child always knew that she had options and because they started her early, she had a good self-esteem without being stuck up.

Addy's mother, Joanie, worked at the local telephone company in their cable TV division. The pay wasn't too bad and she was off on weekends and evenings so she could run her daughter to all of her extracurricular activities. That was Joanie's biggest concern. For the area they lived in, working at the telephone company was nothing to spit at. There were lots worse jobs out there for a lot less money.

Joseph, Addy's father, owned his own construction company: McMullen's Master Construction and they specialized in vinyl siding but dabbled in a little bit of everything. Being from the south, you could always find a construction crew waiting to work so it was a competitive market for Joe. It was also great money when the crew had work to do but there were often times that the construction well ran dry in the surrounding counties. This type of labor drought would force Joseph and his boys to work out of town a lot just to make ends meet.

Joanie was not fond of the times when her husband had to go away for work and Addy could tell when it was coming. Her mom and dad would have little to say to one another for a day or two then her dad was packing up. Addy always thought her father was a good man to make such a sacrifice to provide for them. She wasn't sure why her mother was so unhappy about it, other than missing her husband while he was away.

When Addy was six years old, Joe and Joanie bought a house on Marchess Street in Vigoss and were finally able to move out of their small apartment. This was the street that told everyone "We have arrived." All of Joanie's friends wanted a house on Marchess and now she was actually getting her dream. It was a quiet family neighborhood with spacious homes on little green lots; the kind that would look like they had been cut out with a cookie cutter if you viewed them from the air above. Everyone had their own Bradford pear tree in their yard. It was picturesque.

The payments were a little steep but nothing the young parents couldn't afford if they managed their money well and both of them worked. This was the opportunity for their daughter to grow up on the right side of the tracks. Addy's mother frequently reminded her father of the importance of such things.

What if our drapes are out of style? What if the flowers in our flower bed appear to be less stylish than our neighbors? We may run the risk of being flogged by the home owner's association. Addy found some of her mother's arguments ridiculous but she didn't give those thoughts a voice. To do that would hurt her mom's feelings and she knew that she meant well. Joanie never really seemed materialistic in her daughter's eyes. She did however seem very insecure as Addy got older. She seemed to crave the approval of her friends and fellow neighbors. She was constantly striving for better and encouraged her daughter to do the same.

"You can't settle for second best honey. Addy? Addy? Are you listening to me? Adelicia! I'm speaking to you."

"I'm sorry mom, I'm listening to you."

Frustrated by now, Joanie looked at her daughter and grumbled, "Good. You'll appreciate this advice one day."

Addy never knew another home other than the cozy little house on Marchess Street. She was much too young to remember the little apartment with any clarity. The house on Marchess was her home and the girls on the street had grown to be her friends. It was all as it should be in middle class America.

She could remember evenings when her dad came home before dark. He would come through the house yelling for his 'little punkin pie'. That's what he always called her. She would run into his arms as he lifted her up and swung her around. Then they would usually go outside and throw the baseball or the football. She was content to play like a little boy but enjoyed the tenderness her father lavished on his little girl. Her dad had to be away a lot so he made sure that he did all he could to make up for his absence when he was with his family.

When Addy was about four months shy from her sixteenth birthday, her mother began taking night classes. She had decided she wanted to try her hand at an actual career before she got any older, or so she claimed. Addy didn't think that had much to do with it. Carlie Marcus' mom had begun night classes about a month earlier and the neighborhood was all buzzing about her desire to

23

better her life and how courageous she was. There was NO way Joanie would miss out on all the adulation that Jean Marcus was enjoying as the brave educational pioneer of moms. The day she told her daughter her plans to go back to school at night, Addy actually laughed at her.

"So, you think I can't do it? Is that it? You think Jean Marcus is so much smarter than me? I'm just a stupid woman who deserves to spend her life at the phone company until retirement?"

Her mom was visibly wounded by her reaction.

"No mom, not at all. I think you're the smartest woman I know. I just think sometimes you do things for other people's benefit and not really your own. You know?"

Joanie's brows knitted together.

"No, Adelicia, I don't *know*. What is it that you're saying? I don't really want to go to school? Are you implying that I'm trying to compete with someone, maybe Jean?"

With every word, her mother's voice was getting louder. She had really stuck her foot in her mouth this time. For someone who was such a level headed, strong willed person of determination, her mom could be such a drama queen when she got offended. And it seemed Addy had successfully offended her on this subject. She placed her bowl of cereal down on the kitchen counter as her mother stood in front of her drumming her fingers on the counter, apparently spoiling for a verbal fight. She stretched out her hands, palms up to her mom and bowed in a mocking gesture.

"I'm very sorry mom. I did not mean to upset you. I wasn't implying anything. I just worry that you do too much. You take on too many projects trying to be superwoman and it causes me to worry about you."

This was how it was done. You had to turn the situation where it appeared that you were a doting subject

24

only wishing the best for your most excellent royal highness. This was how you got forgiven in the McMullen household. Joanie's fingers stopped drumming and her face softened immediately.

"Oh sweetie, don't worry about me. I'm going to be just fine. Yes, it will be tiring to work and to go to school but I do it for you and your father. Our family is that important to me."

She reached out and patted Addy's shoulder. Turning to walk away, Joanie was obviously happy again being in typical martyr mode. Addy was comfortable letting her be whatever made her happy.

Joseph had been working out of state for more than a month doing reconstruction on a town that was hit by tornados earlier in the year. It upset him more than he let on to be away from his family but with the construction market going down the tubes in Georgia, he had to make a living somehow. Houses and cars don't pay for themselves.

It wouldn't be long and Addy would be going off to college and that would cost money as well. The money had to come from somewhere. Of course, he also had his men to worry about. They had families that had to eat just like his did. It was his duty to take work wherever he could find it. His own father had often worked out of town but he always knew he did it for him and his brothers. That's what real men do for their family, right?

Abby loved her dad but she was used to his out of town work and it didn't bother her for him to be absent at this point in her life. She had so much in her schedule that she really didn't have time for anything else. Most sixteen year old girls are self-absorbed and Adelicia McMullen wasn't so different. Her world revolved around hair styles, working out, boys and who said what about whom this week. She wasn't disrespectful or unappreciative, just oblivious to the nuts and bolts that kept her world going. Kids often are blind to what adults go through in the real world. Addy was the same. She knew that money didn't come easy and her parents worked hard for her despite their faults. They seemed like two people who had a good life and were happy with what they had built in life.

It took her a while to realize the serious tension between her parents but once she caught wind of it, she could tell that it had been coming on for a while. Slowly she began to wonder why she had not noticed it before.

One evening after school Addy was coming in through the back door. She propped her umbrella against the wall and began to pull off her rain coat. Suddenly she heard voices coming from upstairs. It sounded like mumbling at first but the voices seemed to be getting louder by the minute. This puzzled her. She sat her purse on the counter, shook the dampness out of her hair and moved through the dining room towards the ever increasing voices.

"Are you seriously leaving out again?" Joanie asked the question as if it were so obvious, it required no real answer. "Did you hear me Joe? Do you *ever* hear me Joe?" She was beginning to screech.

Instantly she heard her father begin to talk. His voice was deep and sounded threatening.

"You know Joan, I'm real tired of this game. What more do you want from me? Is the house not enough? Are the credit cards not enough? Let me guess, the school tuition I'm paying just is *not* enough?"

"Screw you Joe! I work too. I contribute to this household just as much as you do!"

"Please…spare me your case. By the time you pay for all of Addy's whims and change our living room *froufrou* every month, you have nothing left!"

That comment struck right to Addy's core. She always thought her father was proud of her accomplishments. She didn't know that he viewed her clubs and sports as a financial strain. Weren't they doing well financially? She had thought that they were but from the sound of this fight, she may have been very wrong. Yes her mom spent more than she should sometimes on home décor. Anyone could see that but she had never given the impression that they couldn't afford it.

Footsteps stomped towards the stairs.

"Go ahead and walk away Joe, like you do every time!"

A door slammed so hard the house shook. Joe came swiftly down the stairs only to run head on into his dumbfounded daughter.

"Baby, how long have you been standing here?"

Addy couldn't speak to him right now. She brushed past her dad and went straight to her room. She needed time to take this whole thing in. It seemed that her parents had a whole other relationship behind closed doors that they didn't show her. Had it always been like this? If not, how long had it been going on?

She expected her father to follow her to her room and beg her to let him explain. He didn't come. Her father must not have mentioned their meeting on the stairs to her mother because nobody brought it up at dinner; as a matter of fact, nothing was ever said about it again.

Joe left out the next morning for Texas. It seemed that another month long job was calling his name. If Joanie noticed her daughter spending more time in her room alone day after day, she didn't address it. It was completely possible that Joanie didn't see it because most days Addy never even saw her mother at all. Dinners became a sandwich alone in front of the TV before heading to bed.

Her dad called her a few times a week to check in but still no confrontation about that day on the stairs. It was clear that no one would be discussing the issue with her. She could've asked but her angry pride kept her from

27

speaking about it. She wasn't a child anymore. Why couldn't they talk with her about whatever problems the family was going through?

It seemed like her family had adopted a new motto: If we pretend it isn't happening, it must not be happening.

Chapter 6

Four weeks had passed since that day on the stairs and things on Marchess Street had changed. It wasn't anything you could put your finger on and say, 'See? There is your change.' It was a feeling, a vacant air in the house where sunshine and love once filled the room.

With Joanie working all day and going to class every evening, the house was often silent. Addy had found herself pulling away from her friends and her club obligations. She began missing practice regularly and avoiding meetings. She feigned sick or used the excuse that she had to take on more responsibility since her mother had begun school at night. That wasn't a complete lie. She was left to keep the house going. It wasn't hard though. When you only have yourself to care for, it's easy.

She would hear her mom come in at all different hours or sometimes not at all. Study groups were dominating what spare time she had and according to Joanie, she was studying like a mad woman. Addy never questioned her about it. She had become uninterested in not only her own life activities but other people's as well.

One day in late April, Addy had caught a ride home from school with a friend. It was a half day at her school and she finished her testing early. Tina Cash who lived two houses down offered her a ride and she gladly accepted. It was a nice spring day but she just wasn't in the mood to walk. The school bus dropped the kids in her neighborhood at the entrance to their community. Normally she had no qualms about walking or jogging a few houses down to get to her home but she just didn't have the energy for it today.

The girls had the radio up and were singing a song they both liked as they turned onto their street.

Addy heard Tina gasp, "What in the hell happened at your house?"

That was a question she would like to know the answer to. Her driveway was filled with police cruisers and a few unmarked units as well. Her mother's car was there, which was unusual at this time of day. It was actually unusual for most times of the day lately.

"What is she doing here instead of work?" Addy mumbled, referring to her mother.

Tina rolled slowly up to the curb in front of the house and asked, "Want me to come in with you?" Tina looked anxious to get the dirt on why police were surrounding her residence. Addy shook her head no and silently opened the car door. She pulled herself out of the car and just stood still on the curb. An awful feeling of dread washed over her and she was feeling very dizzy. She even contemplated turning around and climbing back in Tina's car.

Part of her didn't want to know what the police were doing there. She glanced back; it was no use because Tina had already pulled away from the curb. Addy remained motionless on the lawn for a minute or two

30

trying to collect her thoughts. Time seemed to stand still and her light blue t-shirt had begun to cling to her shoulders with a thin layer of cold sweat. She wiped the palms of her hands on her jeans and kicked a rock absently with the toe of her sneaker.

Why was she afraid to go in her own house? She could see the neighbors gathering on their various porches to see what all the commotion was about. Several of them stared at her intensely. They were probably wondering why she was standing in front of her own home like a statue when there was an obvious issue going on inside; an issue of great importance.

She couldn't fault them for thinking those things. She felt as dumb as she looked but try as she might, her legs were locked. It took all her will power to make her feet move towards that house. She could hear the voices and the radios coming from inside as she got closer. She reached out and turned the knob on her front door. Instantly she was greeted by a tall lanky policeman.

"You are who?" asked this walking Slim Jim as she tried to step through her own front door. Suddenly, before she could identify herself, she heard her mother call out.

"There's my daughter! Oh Addy sweetie! You're here!"

She ran to her daughter and threw her arms around her. Joanie's eyes were red and swollen as well as her nose. Her voice was hoarse and cracking.

"Mom, what's going on? What's happened here?"

It was hard to hide the irritation in her voice. Her home was full of strangers and her mother had quite recently been crying. This meant that there was important news no one had told her yet. That was not a good thing. She pushed her mom back from her at arm's length and knitted her brows together. This was her 'I'm not amused' look and her mother knew it.

"Oh Addy, it's your father. He's gone! He was found dead this morning at his job site. They think it was a heart attack."

Chapter 7

Looking back on it now, she couldn't remember if her mother just blurted it out or if she broke it to her gently. She didn't have a clear recollection of that day. She could only remember up until the moment she heard that her father would never be coming home again. She would never hear him call her his 'punkin pie' or kiss the tip of her nose while wrestling on the sofa or smell his scent when he engulfed her in his big strong arms after returning from a long trip. He wouldn't ever be there again to chase away the monsters in her life or to walk her down the aisle when she met her Mr. Right. He would never see her graduate nor have kids of her own.

Her handsome daddy's shirts would hang unworn in his closet. His favorite coffee mug that she made for him in ceramics class when she was 11 would never be held by him again. His shaving kit and cologne would forever sit useless on the vanity of her parent's bathroom as if waiting for his return any day. The snap shots on the refrigerator of holidays, vacations, and school events attended as a family would be the last of their kind. There would never be any new photos of smiling parents with a smiling daughter.

Tools that were so lovingly used and organized would lie in wait gathering cobwebs in the garage until someone came to take them away to a new home, to someone else's father. To a home where joy still lived. To a life that still had hope in it.

These were the thoughts that bombarded her head in the days that passed slowly and laboriously. It seemed a chore just to awaken in the morning.

Gray was all she could see. The sun had been blackened out by death. She couldn't hear anything except the sound of her father's voice in her ears. She was afraid that if she stopped trying to recall that voice, she would suddenly forget the sound of it. It seemed that the world was going on without her.

Why? Hadn't anyone told all these people that her father was dead? How could they have the nerve to go on with life when her daddy had lost his?

Aunts, uncles, friends, co-workers and a host of others paraded in and out over the next few days. The extended family pretty much planned the entire funeral. Joe's brothers and their wives took care of what needed to be handled. Joanie couldn't plan anything. She was inconsolable. This once strong and capable woman was reduced to rubble. The doctor had prescribed her something to help her sleep and that's exactly what she did.

Guys from Joe's crew and their wives came and cooked. They cleaned up and tried their best to be of help to the family. It was odd to have all these virtual strangers cooking in their kitchen, washing their towels, vacuuming their floors.

Addy smiled and said 'thank you' a lot but stayed in her room as often as she was allowed. She didn't want to participate in this funeral. If she didn't participate, she wasn't required to accept that her sweet daddy was gone forever. That was her plan. She would simply deny this entire ordeal until it passed and Joe returned home.

That plan seemed like it would work until the time came for her Aunt Rhonda to appear in her doorway. Addy knew what she was there for. She was there to tell her she had to get dressed for her father's funeral. She considered refusing but her common sense prevailed. Why make this day any harder than it already was? Today was the day that she had to say goodbye to her dad for the last time.

The coroner suggested a sudden heart attack but no one would know for sure until the autopsy report was released. Addy was angry at the coroner. She was angry that her dad was sick and didn't tell anyone. She was angry that he died alone. How could she go into that funeral home and say goodbye to a man she was angry at? Didn't he get his chance to make it up to his 'punkin pie'?

No. He wouldn't. He would never get that chance and she had to accept that.

Uncle John and Aunt Rhonda had driven Addy to the funeral home. Rhonda was helping her out of the car as she looked around for her mother. She just realized that she had not spoken to her mother since this all began. She didn't see Joanie anywhere. She must be inside, Addy thought.

The trio entered the doors to the main parlor and John guided his niece to a comfortable chair by the most beautiful red and white floral arrangement. She could see him talking to the funeral conductor quietly in the corner. The solemn looking older man nodded, agreeing to whatever her uncle had asked of him. John turned and smiled sympathetically at Addy as he made his way back to her. She noticed her Aunt Rhonda talking with one of her cousins that had just come in.

John squatted down in front of her chair. "Are you ready to go in and see your dad?"

She wasn't sure if she was ready or not. The thoughts of denial were creeping back in but she knew this was no time for that.

"I want to see him with Mommy. Where's she at?"

John paused for a moment and looked down at the floor.

"This whole thing is just too much for Joanie. She is in no condition to be here. We left her at home with her sister Mary. That's why we brought you. Rhonda and I are here for you sweetheart, anything you need. We will go in with you."

What little bit of function her brain still had was firing off in rapid succession. Grief had caused her to lose all social graces as well as tact. Could what she just heard him say really be what came out of his mouth? Surely not.

"Are you telling me that my mother will not be attending my father's funeral? Are you seriously telling me that right now? Right as I'm about to go in and see my dead father, you're telling me that my mother would rather lie in bed and play the victim like she always does?"

Addy didn't even realize she had begun to get louder with each sentence. Everyone had stopped to stare at the girl.

"Addy baby, calm down. This is very hard on your mom. You don't know how it feels to lose…"

At this moment Addy's eyes went wild and her voice rose to a scream.

"I DON'T KNOW? I don't know what it's like to lose what? A father? Someone I love? A brother? A friend? That's right. I'm just a kid to you all but at least I can see that I'm not the only one who's lost someone here. Too bad my mother is too selfish to realize that too."

John didn't know how to respond to her outburst and she didn't give him time if he had wanted to. She spun on her heels and headed for the viewing room. Rhonda and several female family members were hot on her trail.

They found her standing over her father's casket, staring into his face and stroking his cheek. It was heartbreaking to watch this girl who by all accounts was old enough to almost be an adult, carry the look of a wounded child. Nobody dared to approach her for several minutes. Visitors filed past her and patted her shoulder but nobody tried to pull her attention from her last few minutes with her father.

The ceremony lasted about 45 minutes and the attendees filed out row by row to walk into the cemetery where Joe would be lowered into his final resting place. The immediate family sat under the tent while the preacher read the Twenty-third Psalm and led everyone in prayer. This concluded the life of a man who meant so much to so many.

People filed past the family, shaking hands and repeating how sorry they were for their loss. If Addy heard "If you need ANYTHING, you just call," one time, she heard it a thousand. She knew they meant well but she wanted to scream out and say, "I DO need something. I need my Daddy back!"

Only a few of the immediate family remained graveside as they lowered him into the earth. Once the casket was at its maximum depth, Addy stood to her feet. She heard a large shovel of dirt hit his coffin. Her lips went numb and all she could hear was ringing in her ears.

Everything went black.

Chapter 8

She was dreaming. Her father was pushing her on her tricycle and chanting, "Pedal baby girl. Pedal!"

Her laughter was contagious. She could hear the echo of her giggles all around her. The sun was shining so bright she could hardly see in front of her. She could feel the rough sidewalk under her tricycle wheels and the wind in her hair. She cried out loudly, "Daddy, I'm doing it!"

Her younger self turned to see her father but suddenly there was nobody behind her. Where had he gone? Fear rose up in her as she looked down at the handlebars. Instantly there were only ropes in her hands. She wasn't a child anymore. She was her current age and the ropes in her hands were taut. Something was attached to the end of them.

Daddy. It had to be him. She began to pull with all her might as she screamed his name. Dark clouds began to circle her body and she could see a large bird like figure. It hovered above her head. She heard the beast screeching in pain. Slowly piece by piece, the animal began to fall apart. Addy could see the blood. She could smell the blood. As the wings of the beast began to come apart she knew it was about to crash down on top of her. She looked up and tried to see its face. A large talon flailed in the air as if it were trying to grab onto something that would keep it from falling. The face was becoming clearer. The creature was her father.

Her eyes flew open and her heart was beating out of her chest. Her head was resting on her uncle's lap and an ambulance worker was shining a light in her eye.

"Miss, can you hear me? Addy, can you speak to me?"

Her head was throbbing and her hip was burning. She must have fallen on it. How? She didn't remember falling. She remembered the stabbing pain in her chest, that was all. She attempted to sit up, bracing herself on the ground. Her hair had fallen out of the clip that was holding it up. The stray clumps of red showed bits of dirt from the fall. Looking down she could see it was all over the side of her dress too.

Her uncle helped her to sit upright and steadied her as the EMT finished examining her. The man asked her politely to sit where she was while he spoke with her uncle for a moment in private. She could hear their low murmuring but couldn't make out what they were saying. Her head wouldn't stop pulsating as she tried to dust the dirt fragments from her dress.

Look at them, over there talking about her out of earshot. That was really beginning to anger Addy. Everyone thought she was too young, too fragile to handle any of this. She instantly felt aggravated because hadn't she just shown them exactly that? She had blacked out for no reason at all and now she was a dirt smeared mess sitting on the ground while everyone looked on her with pity.

Finally her uncle finished his conversation with the man and he came back to where she sat on the ground.

Her Aunt Rhonda and several other female family members that were still there had congregated around her cooing sweetly about how it was all going to be okay. Oh how she wanted to scream at all of them to go away. That would be mean though. She knew that they were only trying to help the best way they knew how. None of this was their fault. She wished she knew whose fault it was so she could punch them in the eye. She hadn't been raised religious so she wasn't sure if she should be mad at God or at Fate or at the unspecific Universe. All she did know was that she was looking for someone to blame so she could feel better.

They helped her to her feet and attempted to clean her back side. She glanced behind her as they helped her to the car. The men were almost finished covering the hole with dirt. No. It would not be okay Aunt Rhonda, not ever again.

Chapter 9

Addy had no real opportunity to confront her mother when she returned from the funeral and no burning desire to do it even if the option presented itself. She was drained and couldn't muster up anything more than disgust for her mother who was still locked in her room. Her head had told her the whole way home that she was going to burst through that bedroom door and let Joanie have it. It seemed that it wouldn't work out that way once she actually arrived at her house and everyone who didn't live there had departed.

In her heart she knew that this was hard for Joanie too and a little bit of her felt selfish for being so angry at her. Her father had always been her rock and she expected her mother to jump up and fill that gap when she needed her the most but she hadn't. She had known her whole life that her mother was less in control than she appeared to be. It just wasn't an issue when her father was alive. Now it would be a defining factor of their relationship.

Joanie emerged from her bedroom on the third day after the funeral much unlike she had been previously. She was showered, her hair was styled and she had makeup on. She came down the stairs and into the living room. Addy was lying on the couch in her sweats and a tank top watching a talk show with two women who appeared to have the same 'baby daddy'. It took a moment for her to realize her mom was standing there staring down at her but when she looked up she made contact with a pair of steely cold eyes.

"Addy, I'm going out. I need to go straighten things out with my job and my classes. I have to get back on track with life. So do you. I advise you to get up and put on some real clothes."

She stared at Joanie with a contemptuous scowl. Her mother shifted her handbag to her other shoulder and patted her hairstyle, like she was checking for the level of bounce in it.

"*Oh really*? So Mommy, does this mean we get to start picking four leaf clovers and dancing on rainbows?" she answered with mock excitement and wide eyes full of fire.

"Stop that Addy! You will NOT be a smart mouth to me. I've done a lot of thinking these past few days."

Joanie strode over and sat down on the love seat across from her daughter, dropped her purse on the end table and crossed her legs. She leaned forward as she continued to talk.

"Your father handled most of the important things in this house and that included you. I'm not saying you and I don't have a good mother-daughter relationship. I'm just saying that I always knew that Joe was your favorite."

She fired her words at her daughter as if she were accusing her of not loving her enough.

"We can't change what has happened and we are going to have to pick ourselves up and move forward."

Addy sat motionless staring daggers into her mother. How dare she come down here and give her this speech when she hadn't even poked her head into her room in a week to see if her daughter needed her! What kind of mother does that? Now suddenly she was the household inspirational speaker? She felt like her mother was punishing her for being sad that her dad was gone. Where was the mother who escorted her to every team practice, every recital? Addy was staring into the face of a stranger. A stranger she wasn't sure she even liked.

Joanie sighed heavily and shook her head slowly.

"Did the world stop Adelicia? No, it didn't. We cannot either. Do what you're told and when I get home tonight I want to see you showered and changed."

With those words, her mother stood and walked out swinging her purse over her arm as she went. Addy could hear her slam the front door as she left. She was so mad she couldn't think straight. She wanted to punch something or someone. She settled for grabbing a throw pillow and heaving it across the room and into a knick-knack cabinet.

Standing to her feet she noticed the red light on the answering machine blinking 'FULL.' She hadn't been answering the phone or checking the messages. All of her friends had probably called a million times to check on her.

She didn't feel like talking.

Chapter 10

Obviously she had avoided everyone for so long over the course of the death and funeral of her father that when she returned to school the next week everyone avoided her like the black plague.

Maybe it was the grief that showed on her face like gray face paint.

Maybe they just didn't know what to say.

Maybe she was giving off a 'leave me alone' vibe.

Who knew? All she did know was that she had gone from being one of the most sought after girls in school to being solitary and ignored. Even her former coaches hadn't bothered to try and persuade her to rejoin the teams. Her teachers let her know how sorry they were for her loss and encouraged her to come by any time she needed to talk.

As for her so-called friends, it was obvious that grief was something that was considered untrendy in their social circle. She was no longer considered one of them. She was socially on her own according to her regular crowd. The people she had not hung out with in the past were too intimidated to welcome her into their cliques even though they had sympathy for her situation.

One day Addy was sitting on the grass by the football field after school. The weather had gotten much warmer and it would only be a week until summer vacation. She hadn't given summer break a thought. She hadn't made any plans. She had grown fond of being outside alone just spending time in her own thoughts, ear buds in and the breeze on her face. It sure did beat going home to an empty house that only held bad memories of her daddy dying or good memories of her daddy being alive. Either one made her heart ache. She had decided it best to find solace in nature. She wouldn't be missed anyway.

Her mother was back to working days and taking classes at night. If Addy thought she came in late when her dad was around, now Joanie hardly came home at all. The line had been drawn between her and her daughter that day in the living room and suddenly they were on two different planes. Mother and daughter existing in the same home but living so far apart they could've been on different continents. Addy was lonely in her grief that had still not passed. It had gone from a hot searing pain in her chest to a dull ache. If her mother felt the same, she didn't show it.

Addy swayed slightly from side to side as the music from her iPod flowed into her ears. A shadow fell across her head and all at once she realized someone was standing behind her. Pulling her ear buds out, she peered up at an extremely tall and adorable boy. She had recently noticed him around but hadn't caught his name. He had moved to their school right before her father's death.

"Hi. Mind if I sit here?"

Addy looked around the deserted football field as if implying that there were many other places to sit other than with her. He smiled and flipped his auburn hair out of his shining blue eyes. He shrugged and looked helpless like a lost puppy.

She motioned to her right and he quickly chunked his backpack to the ground and sat about three feet from her. She didn't want his company but she had little energy to argue about it.

"I'm Drew," he said as he stuck his hand out waiting for a handshake.

There was an awkward silence as she powered off her iPod and tucked it away in her purse. She turned to the tall young man and noticed his hoodie said Ohio State on it.

"Is that where you're from?" she asked absently without taking his hand. He dropped his unshaken hand into his lap and looked down at his shirt.

"Ohio? No, just a fan. My family moved here from south Georgia early this year."

He continued to smile sweetly at her as if her slightly frosty attitude had not yet chilled his bones.

"You're Addy aren't you?"

She nodded slightly as she stared across the field into the wooded area behind the vacant bleachers. This was her way of showing him that she wasn't up for conversation and wanted to be alone. They must not notice innuendo in southern Georgia, she thought. Suddenly Drew grabbed his backpack and stood up.

"OK. I can see where I'm not wanted. I was hoping to talk to one of the prettiest girls around this lame school but it seems that she has been abducted by aliens and they have taken over her body and stolen her voice. She has been turned into an emotionless little gray girl. I go in peace."

Drew swiveled around on his heel and started up the grassy hill when he heard her say, "Wait. I'm sorry."

He turned to see her standing up facing him. She looked a little embarrassed and a little lost for what to say next but she tried to smile.

"It's nice to meet you Drew. I really am sorry I was rude. I've just had a lot on my mind and well, I'm just sorry. Please, come back and we can talk."

He grinned and headed back down the hill. He wasn't sure that tactic would work but it had and he was definitely grateful. The two of them chatted about music, the classes they have, and who their favorite teachers were. It was the first time since her father had died that she felt remotely normal. It may have even been the first time she had smiled since that awful day.

Drew Neal was tall for sixteen years old. He towered over Addy in his six foot two inch frame making her feel like a dwarf. He was also funny. That day near the football field started a friendship that Addy was beginning to depend on. He was the only person who had truly brought her any comfort in her sadness.

The following week had been the end of the school year and the summer break loomed before them. Her friends had slowly started to come back around but Addy had let them know in no uncertain terms that their rejection had wounded her. She pulled away from them and closer day by day to Drew.

The friendship had blossomed for over a month and both of the kids could tell that the feelings were becoming more than either of them thought they ever would. The couple spent the days at the lake when it was sunny and at the library when it rained. They liked many of the same things and it was never hard to find mutual entertainment. One evening when they were sitting on the merry-go-round in the city park, Addy blurted it out.

"Why haven't you tried to hold my hand or kiss me yet? I mean, you're giving me mixed signals. At least I feel like you are."

The silence was deafening. Panic was setting in on both of them.

"Oh Lord. You don't like me like that do you? I'm so humiliated. Oh Lord." Addy covered her face. He could still hear her mumbling 'Oh Lord'. Drew reached up for her hands and pulled them away from her face.

"It's not that Addy. It's not that at all. I do like you. Hell, I like you A LOT! It's just that I'm trying to take it slow."

She looked at him quizzically.

"I don't understand. We've been hanging out every day for over a month and you haven't even flirted with me. You don't have to say you like me in that way if you don't. It won't hurt my feelings."

Drew knew she didn't mean what she had said. He could see the beginning of tears forming in the corners of her eyes. He had hurt her feelings.

"Addy. I'm a Christian. I'm afraid if I go too fast I won't be able to stop. I want to go slow with you because I really like you and if you are '*the one*' we can move towards dating."

"Well Drew, I'm glad you believe in God but what does that have to do with us dating?"

She was becoming frustrated with his excuses. Why had he been giving her all these vibes if he wasn't into her?

"It isn't about just believing in God. It's about believing in him and believing in his son Jesus Christ and trying to live by his teachings."

It was out there, he had said it. He let the cat out of the bag. He wasn't embarrassed of being a Christian but every time he told a friend or a girl he liked, it was always the same. They would run far away or treat him like he was handicapped. It was very hurtful the way most people his age treated him. He knew it wasn't a popular thing to do but it was something he was trying really hard to follow through with. It certainly was not easy for him.

There were a lot of things he just couldn't participate in like his peers did.

He tried as best as he could to explain to her how he didn't believe in premarital sex and how he hoped that she wouldn't stop hanging around with him. Addy wasn't sure what to think about any of it. It was a foreign subject to her and she wasn't an expert on religion. It sounded very restricting, that was the only thing she was sure of. She wanted him to feel the way she did and if it had to be under his rules, then so be it.

Chapter 11

The kids parted ways around 7:00 p.m. that night and Addy headed home. She had laundry to do and putting it off another day was not helping anyone. She didn't even know if she had another outfit clean in her whole closet. The next morning was Sunday and Drew had invited her to go to church with him and his family. She was a little nervous but secretly a bit excited. She had to wash something proper to wear. She didn't want his family to think she was a full blown heathen.

As she headed through the back yard entrance to her house she noticed a light on in the kitchen. She hadn't left a light on when she went out this morning, she thought. Concerned, she walked quietly around the outside of the house to see if there were any vehicles in the driveway. Her mother was never home at this time. Who could it be? Turning a corner she spotted her mom's car in the garage but she also noticed a small black car parked behind Joanie's.

Now she really *was* intrigued. Her mother was home and she had company. Deciding to go around back and enter through the kitchen she headed towards the patio. As she neared the back door she could see her mother leaning across the kitchen bar laughing and there, sitting on the stool across from her, was a young man who couldn't be much older than Addy judging by his looks.

Whatever he was saying seemed to have her mother in stitches. She also noticed that as Joanie laughed she made a point to dip lower in a way that caused her low cut top to shout 'look at me everyone'. She wasn't sure what in the hell was going on around here but someone was about to tell her one way or the other.

Addy purposely jerked the door handle causing the back door to pop loudly as she entered the room. Joanie physically bolted back from the young man on the stool and shot her daughter a look of surprise.

"Honey, you're home! I wasn't sure if you would be out with friends until late or not."

Addy detected a nervous tremor in her mother's voice. She strolled over to the dinette table and plopped down. She tilted her head and propped it on her right hand, elbow on the table.

"Friends? Haven't you heard mom, I don't have friends anymore? Oh, that's right, you wouldn't know because you don't talk to me anymore."

Addy smiled sweetly, as if she had just told her mother what a lovely top she was wearing. Lifting her sneakered feet up to rest on the dinette table, she brazenly waited for her mother to reply. Joanie slowly closed her eyes and reopened them, obviously attempting to contain her anger in front of the much younger man sitting in their kitchen.

"Oh dear, you're always so dramatic. You know how teenagers are these days Bret," Joanie proclaimed while waving her hand towards her new friend as if they had some private joke and he was the state expert on troubled, dramatic teens. He certainly could've passed as an expert on teenagers since it was clear he had been one not long ago.

It was also clear that this 'Bret' seemed amused by this tit for tat between mother and daughter. He kept a vague smirk on his face but his eyes danced with laughter. It was making Addy mad at them both. Joanie had not spoken three words to her in months and now she wanted to act as if she had a direct line to her daughter's personality.

Not in this lifetime.

"Bret, this is my daughter Adelicia. We call her Addy. She's normally not so rude when meeting new people."

Joanie was talking about her as if she weren't even in the same room and this Bret person couldn't stop watching her every move as if waiting for her to jump up from the table and body slam her mother right there on the kitchen floor. Addy stood up and waggled her fingers in Bret's direction as if halfheartedly waving and left the room. She thought she wanted to know what was going on but she realized she couldn't stand to be in the same room with her own mother for more than two minutes. She had to get out of there.

Addy lay across her bed and cried. In less than a year her family had fallen apart completely. She lost her dad, her friends and basically her mom. Thank goodness she had Drew. What would she do without him? Jump off of a bridge is what she would do. She would refuse to think about the state of her miserable home life anymore today, she vowed.

She had gathered up all of her dirty laundry into three baskets and was trying to maneuver them down the stairs all at once when she heard a car start up outside. A badly stained ankle sock fell off the mound in one of the baskets and landed on the stair. She struggled to pick it up without dropping the rest of her load as the sound of the vehicle quickly died away. Her mom and that Bret boy must have decided she wasn't hospitable enough and left. Good riddance. She couldn't tolerate any more fake smiles today.

'It's just you and me dirty laundry,' she thought.

Chapter 12

Her mother and her friend never returned that night. Addy realized this when she got up the next morning to get ready for church with Drew's family. Before she had gone to bed the night before she calmed down and decided she would try to mend fences with her mom as soon as she got home. She waited up as long as she could but Joanie never came so Addy had decided to go ahead and get some sleep.

She showered and dressed in a simple yellow sundress and pulled a light green cardigan over it for modesty. When she had her hair pinned back she decided she would grab a bite to eat before Drew's family arrived to pick her up. In the kitchen, Addy plucked a couple of frozen waffles out of the mini freezer and deposited them into the toaster. While the waffles were warming she opened the pantry to grab the syrup.

Pop went the toaster as it spit out her previously frozen breakfast. She twisted the lid on the syrup but it wouldn't open. She twisted harder but to no avail. The syrup had collected under the cap causing it to be stuck tight. She looked around for something to help her get a grip on the lid. Addy rummaged through a couple of the drawers in the kitchen looking for anything that might be of use. The last drawer she opened was brimming full of envelopes that flew all over the floor at her feet. It reminded her of the 'can of snakes' you could buy in the gag shops.

Syrup would have to wait because she had to clean the mess up before she left or her mom would come home eventually and see it. She didn't want to cause any more reasons for confrontation. If she wanted to clear the air between the two of them, she had to start making more of an effort. Addy was picking up each envelope and creating a stack that would go back into the drawer. When she had almost every envelope picked up, she noticed most of them had a big red stamp on the front. Delinquent, it said.

She started opening the mail one by one and realized they were stacks of overdue bills. The bills were everything beginning with the house payment and down to the cable bill. From the looks of it, Joanie hadn't paid much of anything since Joe had died. The most recent notice from the bank stated that they had fifteen days to vacate the house because it was being foreclosed on.

That notice was sent three days earlier. By her calculations, they now had twelve days to vacate the only home she had ever known. She was sure her mother had said absolutely nothing about this to anyone in the family. If so, she would have heard about it. Considering she wasn't talking to Addy, she didn't tell her anything about it either.

This was unreal. There had to be a mistake. Didn't her father leave them a life insurance policy? She could've sworn he had one because her mother and he were discussing it one night several years ago when she overheard them.

55

A car horn honking outside startled her and she realized Drew was there to pick her up. She hadn't even touched her food. The waffles sat cold in the toaster slots. She didn't have time to do anything about this right now. She would deal with it when she got back. She grabbed her house keys and darted out the door to her ride.

Drew's family was very nice to her. They didn't talk much but they seemed to be friendly. It didn't take more than ten minutes to reach their church, across the bridge in Polton County. It was a large cathedral type church with dark oak pews and stained glass windows all around the sanctuary. The Neal family filed one by one into a pew near the front of the church.

Addy felt a little uncomfortable. She had only attended church a few times in her life and it was usually on a holiday and with a family member. Uncle Barry and his wife had taken her to Glory Presbyterian Church near their house one Easter when she was nine. It was very intimidating for her and it made her feel itchy all over.

That was sort of the way she was feeling now. She wanted to scratch and wiggle but she felt like if she did, everyone would point and stare. She tried to sit still. Funny how the more you try to be still, the more your nose itches or your foot won't stop bobbing on reflex. An older lady in a light purple skirt suit shuffled by their pew and smiled at Mrs. Neal.

"Good to see ya sweetie," she called out.

"It's good to see you this morning Miss Martha. You look lovely today," Drew's mom replied. The lady nodded as if she already knew how lovely she was and needed no affirmation.

As more people filed in, Drew's parents exchanged pleasantries with many others and several of them asked Drew who his friend was. She was introduced and surveyed by each one of them. It was clear to her that

Drew didn't make a habit of bringing girls to church with him. She felt like a new attraction at a three ring circus.

After what seemed like an hour of polite head nods, perfunctory hand waves and such, the reverend appeared at the front of the church in his dark suit with his gray hair neatly combed over in a covert attempt to cover what was surely a balding spot right at the very top of his head.

"Good morning ladies and gentlemen. It's good to see everyone here this beautiful morning. We are lucky to have another day to visit the house of God."

A few 'amens' sounded from the opposite side of the auditorium. He opened his bible that lay on the podium in front of him and began his opening prayer with the congregation. Drew reached over during the prayer and laid his hand on Addy's. It surprised her enough to make her open her eyes. She quickly closed them, concerned with being stricken down for interrupting a prayer by looking up.

She wondered why people closed their eyes to pray. Was it a rule in the Bible? Was God waiting for their eyes to be closed so he could sneak in the back of the church and watch to see who was good and who was bad? Did opening your eyes make him go away? Were these questions ridiculous? She dared not ask anyone, especially Drew.

While her mind was wandering, she imagined buying a book at the local Walmart called "The Bible for Dummies". The thought almost made her giggle out loud. She really never realized how much she *didn't* know about church. Her grandparents on her father's side of the family went to church but they didn't visit very often. They also had never offered to take Addy with them. In the south most people just assume people know who God is and how he works. The ones who know all about it don't usually stop and think maybe others don't know. The ones who don't know are usually too unconcerned or too embarrassed to ask what all the fuss is about. It could often be a lose-lose situation.

The reverend concluded his prayer and the choir sang several songs. The music was lovely and it actually reduced the anxiety she was feeling. At least the hand that Drew was holding was no longer sweating like a pig in July. She kept trying to wipe it on her dress without him realizing what she was doing.

Drew however was cool as a cucumber. She could tell he was totally at home in a church environment. His face seemed to light up more with each word the reverend spoke. His gaze was one of concentration and rapt attention. It had been so long since Addy had seen or felt the type of happiness that showed on Drew's face. She was surprised to realize that she secretly felt envious of him. In her heart she wished there was something in her life she could anchor herself to like Drew had. She didn't really understand it, but something deep inside of her was yearning to connect to whatever this was. She was glad she had gone with them this morning.

Chapter 13

Bret pulled up in the driveway at 200 Marchess Street to let Joanie McMullen out of his car. He put the car into park and looked over at the much older lady in his passenger seat.

"Do you plan on telling your daughter about us today or will you be avoiding it until the last minute?"

He held his finger up like he had just remembered something very important.

"I know, you can surprise her with a moving truck that says 'Congratulations you're moving out and getting a new stepdad'!"

Joanie swatted at him as he laughingly teased her.

"Don't joke Bret. She isn't going to take it well when I tell her we're losing the house. She's going to be less happy when I tell her about us. She's been a different girl since Joe died. We don't communicate anymore. I don't know where to start," she said as she dropped her head and held her hands up in a motion of surrender. "I know that doesn't matter though. I have to deal with it today. The moving trucks are coming tomorrow and time for dilly dallying has run out."

With that, she leaned over and gave Bret a long slow kiss. As their lips parted she whispered, "I love you baby."

Bret smiled at her and whispered in return, "I love you too Mrs. Thomas," as he playfully tapped her on the tip of her nose.

She jumped back and said, "Oh Bret, I told you not to say that around Addy until I can tell her. There's enough to unload right now without having to spill the beans and tell her we have already married. She doesn't even know you yet."

"I know, I know. Don't worry. My lips are sealed for now." He winked slyly at her.

Joanie opened the car door and got out. She dug through her purse for the door keys and when she finally found them wedged under her sunglasses, she unlocked the door and went in. She yawned. It was close to lunch time and she was already tired. Having a new younger husband was more work than she remembered. Sleep was something she didn't get often.

Depositing her handbag and keys on the table in the foyer, she headed for the kitchen for a glass of juice. Walking in, she noticed a pile of papers on the counter and waffles still in the toaster. What was wrong with that girl? She usually wasn't this messy. Joanie placed the syrup back in the pantry then took the waffles from the toaster and threw them in the trash can.

That was when she noticed the bills on the counter.

Oh dear God. Addy saw them. Now what would she say? She would look like a liar. Joanie walked over to the dinette and sat down, defeated. She really did want to reach out to her daughter after Joe died but she was just so devastated she couldn't. She and Joe were having problems when he left and it made her feel so guilty that their last words were in anger. If the truth were told, their problems had started long before he left for his last trip and they were only months away from a possible separation, a permanent separation.

That didn't make it any easier to lose her husband this way. It wasn't supposed to be like this. Not for her. Not for Addy. Joe would be ashamed of the way she had treated their daughter but Addy was born strong, not like her. She could see that from day one. Addy would be fine. She would pull herself up. She was sure of that. It was her who needed support.

Thank God she had found Bret. He was her saving grace.

Bret Thomas was a 25 year-old website designer who had recently graduated college and was fortunate enough to meet Joanie McMullen one day while coming out of the corner convenience store. She had been walking in as he was going out and she dropped her cell phone. He reached to pick it up for her. He could tell she was a bit older than him but she was a very pretty lady. He didn't realize at first that she was over ten years his senior.

Obviously just leaving work she still had on her suit jacket with her pencil skirt. He saw the white name plate on her lapel that simply said 'Joanie'. Her dark red hair was long and wavy. He could tell she had recently taken it down from some type of knot and it flowed beautifully around her shoulders. He just couldn't resist.

"Wow. I don't mean to be forward but you are truly gorgeous. Do you model?"

It was a crappy pick up line and she knew it but for some reason it still made her blush.

"I'm sorry, I don't model. It seems your luck has run out."

She took her phone from his hand and walked in the store, not looking back. He could feel a challenge coming on. He followed her back in the store.

"What do you mean my luck has run out?" he asked her lightly.

"I mean, if you're looking to run into a model in a convenience store, today isn't your day," Joanie replied.

"I think it is."

She wanted to dislike this young man in front of her but he was so upbeat and blunt she just couldn't bring herself to hold onto her mad face. She smiled and started to laugh.

"There it is," he said. "There's the beautiful smile I knew was under that scowl I got before."

Bret followed her out to her car and introduced himself. He had also asked her out to dinner and surprisingly enough, she accepted. Neither of them could believe she had accepted. Joanie had been a wife and a mother for so long she forgot that she was even considered attractive, especially to someone his age. Bret, who was normally great with the girls, had never taken a shot at an older woman and was very surprised that she gave him the time of day.

It wasn't hard for Joanie to be persuaded after getting a good look at Bret. His midnight black hair and dark eyes suited him perfectly. He had light olive skin and was a little over six feet tall. He looked like someone who ran track or regularly worked out at the gym. There weren't many women around who would say no to that.

The problem was that she happened to be married. Bret had come along several months before Joe's death.

The chance meeting had come on the heels of one of Joe and Joanie's frequent fights. Harsh words had been thrown around the night before and the frustration had mounted. Bret had appeared at just the right interval to slide into her life.

She had never cheated on Joe in the past, never even considered it but lately the thought had popped up every time there was a new fight. Nights alone when Joe was out of town didn't help matters. Addy was older now and had her own social life. Joanie felt isolated and left behind with a husband who had grown cold and a life that was far less than fulfilling. That was why she started night classes in the first place. She wanted something strictly for herself just this once. They made fun of her for worrying about things like decorating the house and manicuring the lawn but that was her way of doing her part for them all to have a better life. The problem was that her daughter was more like her husband than she would have liked to think. Joanie was the odd one out.

The first date with Bret changed all of that. She suddenly remembered what it felt like to be wanted, needed. He made her feel important. He listened to her. He wanted to know her. She knew it was wrong and the guilt was killing her but she told herself it was one innocent dinner and she would never see him again.

It didn't turn out that way. When he called on her a few days later she found herself skipping her classes after work to meet him at the movies or to have dinner. Often times they would just meet at his place for pizza and a movie. After a month of harmless dating passed, he asked her to go to a play in the city and suggested they stay overnight in a hotel. Joe was away again and things were at an all- time low between the two of them. She was no fool. She knew what she was agreeing to when she said yes but she couldn't stop herself from wanting it.

The entire night had been heavenly and the thought of going home to a husband who was only present on a telephone was no longer enough. She decided she would tell Joe how she felt when he returned. Addy would turn against her and side with her father. That was a fact. It hurt her deeply to know her daughter would resent her but she was beyond the point of turning back now. Addy was almost grown and she had been a good mother to her in all ways. She would just have to understand that sometimes grown-ups divorce. That was the bottom line.

When Joe returned from his trip three weeks later it took two days to get him to give her a moment of his time. She intended to tell him she didn't love him anymore. Before she could get to the heart of the matter with him, he told her he was leaving for another out of state job the next day. She exploded. He couldn't pay her enough attention for her to tell him she wanted to leave him. Joanie was furious. She screamed. He screamed. In the end, he packed his things and left that night. That was the last time she saw her husband alive.

Chapter 14

Joanie was still sitting at the dinette thinking about how she was going to deliver the news to her daughter when Addy came home. She looked up to see her standing in the doorway just staring at her with the strangest look on her face.

"Sit down Adelicia. I'm not fighting with you. I know you're mad. I know you saw the foreclosure notices. Yes, I should've told you before now but I didn't and here we are. You need to know our situation and I need for you to be adult about this whole thing. There's no place for childish tantrums any longer."

Addy yanked out the kitchen chair, pulled off her green sweater and draped it over the back before she sat down. She spread out her hands, palms up as if to say 'let's have it'.

"Your father left us barely enough life insurance to pay for the funeral. It cost a small fortune to have his body shipped home. The rest of the money went to pay a few small loans we had taken out just to keep afloat. I don't make enough money to afford this house or the car.

I've done the best I could to keep our electricity on, pay our phone bill and put food on the table. The bank is taking this house. There will be a moving truck here in the morning to pack all of our things and put them into storage for now."

There was a long pause when Joanie stopped talking. Tears were welling up in her daughter's eyes. She wasn't sure if they were due to sadness or anger or both. Her small fists were clenched so tightly on the table she could see her white knuckles.

"Where will we go? Where are we supposed to live? This is our home. Can't they give us extra time to catch up what we owe? Didn't you tell them Daddy died? What about your schooling?"

Desperate to find a solution, Addy's mind was racing.

"The bank knows our situation and they have already been more generous than they had to be. I simply cannot afford this place. We will be going to Bret's house. We are moving in with him."

There, she had said it.

"Bret? You mean that little boy who was here yesterday that you were ridiculously throwing yourself at? You must be joking. Why would we move in with him? Do his mommy and daddy know we're coming?" she spat sarcastically.

This conversation would only go down-hill from here, Joanie thought.

"For your information young lady, Bret does not live with his parents. He has his own home here in Despin County and he is a website designer for a marketing firm. He has a very nice home and is quite well off for someone his age; which is 25."

This was becoming more bizarre to Addy with each new revelation. Breathe, she told herself. This must be what it felt like to hyperventilate. Her lungs were constricting and she was having trouble breathing deeply.

"Mother, I'm not going to ask you again. Tell me why you think it's appropriate for us to be moving in with this person. I mean, why not Grandma and Grandpa or Aunt Linda? They all have big houses with extra room. I don't understand."

It was clear that she had no chance of moving this conversation along unless she leveled with Addy.

"First of all, I have no desire to move out of the county and if we lived with any of those people you named, we would have to do just that. Second, Bret is a wonderful person and has a gorgeous home with plenty of room. Lastly, we will be moving to his home because it is our home too. He and I are married Addy. He is my husband and your step-father."

The girl visibly recoiled from shock. Tears began streaming down both sides of her face. She began to shake her head back and forth as if denying any further information.

"Don't start this Addy. You're not a child anymore. Your father is gone. Bret is a great person who loves me and can provide for us. Give him a chance to love you too. I just know you will feel the same when you get to know him."

Addy jumped up from the table knocking her green sweater to the floor and ran. She ran out the door and down the sidewalk. She ran out of their neighborhood and kept running until her lungs burned and her side had a stitch in it.

She found herself in front of Drew's house. She was dripping with sweat and her cotton sundress was clinging to every inch of her. Tears continued to pour down her face and run down the front of her dress. She stood at his mailbox not knowing what to do next when Drew raced out his front door.

"Addy! What happened? Are you alright? Sit down," he ordered as he helped her to sit on the curb. He sat beside her and put his arm around her shoulders. She

67

sobbed heavily in his embrace until she felt like she had run dry. He waited patiently until she calmed down before he asked softly, "Please tell me what has you so upset."

She unloaded all of it. She told him how she had found the hidden mail, how she had been confronted by her mother and how she had a new life all in the last thirty minutes. When she was finished with her story she looked up at him helplessly and whispered, "Help me Drew. I don't know what to do."

He couldn't imagine being in her shoes. He felt so bad for her but he didn't know what advice he could give her that would magically make all the pain go away. He thought a minute and looked her straight in the eye.

"I don't have the answers Addy but I know who does. God is the only one who can help you with this, with your pain. You have to give it to him."

She began to cry again. "But I don't know how," she wailed.

"Shhh. Don't cry, I will pray for you if it would help." She vigorously nodded her head yes.

"Dear Lord, we come to you today to thank you for all your many blessings. We thank you that you love us enough to forgive us when we make mistakes and love us when we are unlovable. God we ask you to touch Addy. Help her with her family issues and heal the pain that she carries deep inside of her. Help the bad things in her life to work out for her good. We thank you in advance for all that you do. Amen."

She looked up at him and asked in a small voice, "Why did you thank him in advance?"

He smiled at her and said, "That's faith at work. We thank him before he does it because we have faith that it will happen. It tells him that we know that he is who he says he is and can do what he says he can do."

The crying had subsided and Drew had offered for her to come inside but she declined. She knew she had to go home and face her life. She couldn't run away forever. There was a new resolve inside of her that made her want to try to make the best of a horrible situation. She couldn't explain the sudden realization; she only knew she wasn't meant to fight it anymore. She had to go home and do what must be done.

Drew went in and told his parents that he was taking her home. They walked and talked more about what life would be like for her now in a new home with a new man in her family. Drew just continued to encourage her and tell her she would only be across town. He advised her to keep praying because God was always listening.

At her back door, he hugged her tightly and kissed her forehead. They said goodbye and she entered her home just in time for her very last sunset on Marchess Street.

Chapter 15

When the moving van showed up the next day Addy had her entire room ready to go. She hadn't spoken with her mother since she ran out on her the evening before. She just didn't know what to say. Sometime silence was the safest road to take until you were sure which side you should be driving on.

Bret had shown up early at day break and she could hear the two of them directing the movers where to put what on the truck. Some things were going to his house and others would be going into storage. His house, not their house. *This* was her house. His house might be her mother's home someday soon but it would never be hers.

When most of the house had been emptied and the men had carried all of her belongings out of her room and down the stairs, she emerged from her bedroom one last time. She could still see her father standing in this doorway calling out to her, "Goodnight punkin pie. I love you the mostest." To which she would giggle and reply, "Nope. I love *you* mostest Daddy!" A tear dripped on her wrist and she realized she was crying. She could hear

70

him shouting into her closet saying, "Okay closet monsters, hear this! You get out of this closet right now or I will personally turn our pet dragon loose on you and he will barbeque your behind!"

The memories made her chuckle. Her father, her protector. She would stash all of these memories deep in her heart so that when she couldn't be here where she still felt him, she could remember him just as much.

Addy closed the door on the bedroom that saw her happiness and her tears. She moved down the hall towards the stairs. Something compelled her to stop one last time at her parents' bedroom for a final look. It was strange to see it empty. Other people would come soon and fill the rooms with their own furniture and their own memories. It would be as if they never lived here. She began to back out of the doorway when she noticed something still in the closet. Walking over she could see through the crack in the door. It was her father's clothing, still hanging in his closet. Joanie intended to leave it all. Common sense told her there was no need to bring it with them but that didn't make it feel any less like a betrayal to her. She reached inside and pulled an old worn flannel work shirt off of the hanger and held it to her face.

It still smelled like him just a little. She knew that smell would go away soon but she couldn't resist snuggling it to her cheek. This one shirt was going with her. The rest could stay. They would probably be taken to Goodwill by the next people who live here. As for this particular shirt, it would be going with her to comfort her when she missed him. She pushed her arms into the oversized sleeves and immediately had to roll up the cuffs to keep from losing her hands inside them.

It felt good to have his shirt on. She felt closer to him on this day. It was what she needed to be able to close the door on this part of her life and head into something new.

Chapter 16

She exited the house through the front door. Her mother and Bret were standing at the truck talking with the movers. Joanie turned to her daughter, surprised to see that she was wearing one of Joe's old work shirts. She chose to ignore that fact. This would not be a day of fighting but a day of joy for their exciting new life. She would finally be able to give her daughter such a great future instead of worrying about how she would pay for even the most basic needs. If only Addy could see it that way, she thought.

One day she *would* see it and she *would* thank her mom for being smart about their futures. Joanie was sure of it.

Everyone followed one another like a funeral procession away from Marchess Street and towards their new destination. Addy was riding in the car with her mom. Bret was behind them in his little black sports car and the moving truck was leading the pack. It took about twenty minutes to get across town. They passed her high school as well as the hardware store. About a mile further they took a right turn onto a road that had a large yellow 'Dead End' sign at the entrance. She had seen this road many times in her life but never entered it for any reason. There's something about a dead end sign that makes somebody wonder what's waiting at that particular dead end. It just feels ominous.

It was a small black top road with large and lush green pastures on both sides. About a quarter of a mile down they passed a drive way with a large mail box shaped like a log cabin. It had a number 32 on it and a small sign hanging on the little cabin porch that read 'The Hastings Family'. Their driveway was so long that you couldn't see the actual house from the road. She could only see the tree line where their driveway bent behind and disappeared.

The road continued for another half mile until the end was visible. It circled into a cul-de-sac and there was a paved driveway in the center that was large enough for two cars to pass going opposite directions. To the right of the entrance was a granite monument that read 'Rolling Hills Estate' and below it in smaller lettering it said 'Thomas Family'. There were trees and pastures etched into the stone. It was beautiful, she had to admit.

Wow, she thought, his home has its own name; impressive to say the least. How well off was this new stepdad of hers? Crazy how she was headed to a home she knew nothing of with a man she knew nothing about.

With the large truck in front of them it was hard for Addy to see a far distance out front. When they followed the truck into the wide driveway she tried in vain to see around its girth but all she could see was pasture. The drive suddenly turned to the right , heading up an incline and she had full view as they continued behind the truck. Amongst beautifully manicured lawns there were Japanese maple trees and dogwood trees surrounded by flower beds in which bloomed a full array of colors. On the north side of the house she could see a massive weeping willow tree with a wrought iron picnic table underneath. There were shrubs and fruit trees everywhere she looked and right in the center of it all was a large two-story brick house.

It had an expansive front entryway with elaborate brick stairs that led up to the veranda. Large pillars supported the roof of the veranda and ran the length of the entire front of the home just like the old southern plantation houses. Several large oak rocking chairs beckoned from the whitewashed decking. The modern touch was that she could see ceiling fans every ten or fifteen feet on the veranda making it possible to enjoy an evening outside even if no breeze was blowing.

The moving truck backed to the front door, preparing to relocate their belongings to the new home. When the car was parked, Joanie glanced over at her daughter with a look of complete satisfaction and said, "Didn't I tell you he was well off?"

Addy nodded her head in agreement. Her mother jumped out quickly and ran to the front door to begin ordering the men where to unload their possessions. Unsure of what to do next, Addy remained seated in the car. She jumped as her door opened unexpectedly and Bret was standing by her side.

"Your mom is busy with the movers so I thought I would be the one to escort you into your new home. I hope it meets your approval so far."

It did. It really did. She hadn't wanted to like any place other than her own home but so far she was awestruck by the opulence around her. She always felt privileged to live in their old home which, by most people's standards, was well off. This house had to be five times the square footage of the old house. She could only imagine what the inside looked like.

"Does website design really pay this much?" she asked cautiously.

He laughed lightly. "No, unfortunately not. My Grandfather was in the cattle business and he made quite a bit of money before he was thirty. He invested that money well. He also branched out and opened a meat packing business in Atlanta to which he and a few of his rancher friends were the main suppliers of beef. The Hastings next door, their family were partners in it all. The meat packing plant was sold when I was really young but the investments my Grandpa made paid off better than anyone could have guessed. Needless to say, we don't have cows anymore but I have a very impressive trust. I also receive a monthly stipend from several long term investments."

Addy realized her mouth was agape. She closed it quickly and tried to hide the look of shock.

"So, where are your parents now? I mean, Mom said you don't live with them. Are they dead? I'm sorry, that was rude. I shouldn't have said it that way."

The grin on his face showed he wasn't offended at all. This was the most conversation he had been offered yet by his new step-daughter and he was happy for it.

"No, they aren't deceased. They are much older though. They were both in their forties before I was born so they are past retirement age. They bought a condo in Florida and moved down about two years ago. They left me with the house since I am the only child of the oldest son."

Bret extended his hand to her and bowed saying, "Since you now know my entire family history, would like to see the inside of your new home?"

Taking his outstretched hand, she climbed out of the vehicle. Bret escorted her up to the veranda, all the while telling her how many acres their land was and all the different spots that were a 'must see'. He told her of a pond and a small creek as well as the best place to watch the deer play in the evenings. According to Bret, even wild turkeys congregated in the back yard during their prime season.

Addy felt guilty for feeling excited about this place. She wanted to hate it. She wanted to hate him. So far, she could hate neither.

The two entered the house to hear Joanie faintly yelling, "No, those boxes go over here, not there. Just sit them down and I will unpack them myself."

The foyer was a huge cavern of a room. She guessed that the ceiling must be twenty-five feet high. To the right there was a semi-circle staircase that started at the bottom far right of the room and wound slowly up, curving to the left and ending at the second floor. The banisters were ornately carved cherry wood polished to perfection. Addy thought she could imagine a princess standing on such a staircase with her gown flowing out behind her.

As if Bret could read her thoughts he said, "My mom always said it was a staircase built for a princess. What do you think?"

"I think it's beautiful. Too bad you won't have a daughter of your own one day to play princess on them."

Why had she said that? How insensitive of her.

Bret gave her a puzzled look and replied, "Your mom isn't too old to have more children. It is still a possibility."

Addy flushed thinking about her mother having another baby. Why didn't that occur to her before now? What would happen if her mom and Bret were to have a little one of their own? Where would that leave her and her mom? She would be the odd one out. The thought suddenly darkened her mood. There was the guilt again. Who was she to begrudge this handsome and sweet guy a child of his own? She was almost seventeen now and she had to have a more adult outlook on life. If there was to be another baby, she would have to be happy for them. She wished Drew were with her through this first day. It would make her feel so much calmer. He had that effect on her.

"You're right. I'm sorry. I just wasn't thinking."

He led her into the sitting room. She knew it must be a sitting room because there were no televisions or stereos, only a large bookcase, two matching sofas, a small love seat and one high backed chair. There were several end tables as well as a coffee table. It all looked very elegant, especially with the huge fireplace. It wasn't a traditional wood burning fireplace but instead had a large gas log configuration. She could see herself cuddled up on a cold winter day with the fireplace and a good book right here on this sofa. Bret motioned for her to sit down.

"Before we see the rest of the house I think you and I need to clear the air. Have a seat."

She knew this was coming eventually. He was about to give her the rules of the house talk or something like that. She sat down on the loveseat closest to the door and he sat down beside her. It was a bit unnerving to be this close to her mother's new husband. She could smell his pricey cologne.

"I know this has been hard for you and I know that it's strange to see your mom with someone other than your dad, especially someone who isn't a whole lot older than you. I just want you to know that it's cool if you need time to get used to me. I won't push you. I just want to be friends and hopefully one day you will think of me as family. My home is your home. I mean it, anything you need. I'm here for you and your mom."

She could see the sincerity in his dark eyes.

"Thank you Bret. That means a lot".

Addy stood up quickly. She had to move away from him, the closeness was beginning to make her claustrophobic.

"Well, with that out of the way, let's see the rest of the house and find your mother. Maybe she hasn't driven the movers away with a headache." Bret laughed at his own joke and they headed out.

Chapter 17

The rest of the house was just as amazing as she imagined it would be. In addition to the foyer and the sitting room there were six other rooms downstairs. The enormous kitchen was outfitted with professional grade appliances and the formal dining room easily seated twelve. The lower level bathroom was the largest Addy had ever seen. A cavernous room, specifically designed for entertaining, seemed to take up half the downstairs area. There was also a bright fitness room set up to rival a small commercial gym and Bret's spacious home office.

The upstairs was equally fabulous with five bedrooms, each with their own full bath and walk-in closet with a dressing room. Two of the bedrooms even had their own sitting rooms. Her room was to be at the very opposite side of the upstairs from her mother and Bret's room. She was grateful for that. She didn't know how much she could handle accidentally hearing anything that may be going on in there. The thought turned her stomach.

Addy knew her mother was a very pretty woman but she *was* curious as to what made such a handsome and obviously wealthy young guy like Bret want to be with her. Joanie was broke, widowed and saddled with a teenage daughter. That couldn't have been a selling point for him. She would like to be able to say it was her mom's winning personality but she had always felt her mom to be a bit too whiny and insistent with her dad. Maybe she was a completely different person with Bret. Who knew? Maybe he just had mommy issues since his parents were so much older than him. Maybe it's true what they say about how you can't choose who you love. It just happens. She wondered if she and Drew would get to that point.

She really did like him and she already knew she had deep feelings for him but she wasn't sure yet if it was love. She really wasn't sure what real love felt like. Before her father died she would host sleepovers with her girlfriends and they were always talking about being in love with this boy or that boy and of course it was scandalous to talk about; but deep down she wondered how all of her friends could fall in and out of love so often. Wasn't love a permanent thing? She always thought that when she fell in love it would be forever.

Maybe that was a childish way of thinking. Maybe love really was limited. Look at her parents. They were on the verge of divorce when her dad died. Their love had seemed unbreakable to her but in reality, it was slowly dying for a long time. Real love was way more complex than movies made it out to be. It was her opinion that it was best to handle any type of love with caution.

She entered her new bedroom to find all of her boxes stacked neatly in her sitting room. Her room was one of the two with a sitting room attached. She had protested when Bret first showed her but he insisted that every lady needed a sitting room.

"Why do I need a sitting room in my bedroom?" she asked him, sincerely wanting to know the answer. She was staring at him wide eyed waiting for the information that would tell her how important this area was for her womanhood.

Bret put his forefinger to his lip as if searching for the right explanation.

"Well, you need it for, uhm, sitting I guess. Heck I don't know what you girls need half the things you need for. All I know is your mom said you need it."

They both burst out laughing.

"So be it. I will graciously accept your sitting room," Addy curtsied in mock allegiance as if bowing before royalty.

"Very well my lady. I shall retire to my quarters and allow you your privacy," Bret joked in a fake and badly dictated British accent.

She giggled as he backed out of the door with a small salute. This might not be so bad after all, she mused. The sitting room before her had lightly colored wood paneled walls with a small gas log fireplace like she saw downstairs, only not as big. She had a leather sofa with a coffee table in front of the fireplace. The table had two books on it. One was a collection of pictures depicting the finer art collections in the world. The other book was a historical account of the history of music beginning with the Baroque period.

To her right was a large oak cabinet that held a set of folding doors in the center. When the doors were opened they revealed a 42-inch flat screen TV, DVD player and a Bose stereo system. In front of this cabinet was an oversized leather recliner that matched the sofa.

Turning to her left was a door that opened into the bed chamber area. Entering the doorway, she was surprised to see that this room seemed even larger than the previous one. There was a king-sized canopy bed in the center of the room. The canopy was made of peach colored translucent mesh fabric. The fluffy down comforter was a pale lilac with tiny peach colored flowers grouped in patterns. The rug matched the bed linens as well.

Behind the bed were tall floor to ceiling bay windows with ivory and peach linen drapes. You could see out across the pasture all the way to the tree line of the woods. It was a beautiful view.

Straight ahead was the entrance to her personal bathroom which was equipped with a walk-in shower and a separate whirlpool tub. A large beveled mirror ran the length of the double vanity. She could also access her walk-in closet and dressing room from the bathroom or the bedroom, either one.

She felt like a princess. How would she ever fill all this space? She ducked her head into her closet and flipped on the light. There were clothes in it. Had they made a mistake and put her in someone else's room? Whose clothes were these? She started to back away when she realized that they all still had price tags on them. These clothes were all new. There were at least twenty outfits hanging up, not counting the shoe boxes that sat on the floor.

"Addy! Where are you dear? Addy?" Joanie was shouting for her from the outer room.

"I'm in here Mom!" Addy shouted back.

Gliding into the room and up to the closet door, her mother carried a look of total contentment on her face. Her jeans were dusty and her t-shirt was a bit stained from all the unpacking but Addy thought her mother looked younger than she had ever remembered seeing her. The long silky hair that her daughter had always envied was balled up into a knot on the back of her head. It gave her the look of a ballerina. For a split second Addy could see exactly why Bret had fallen for her mother.

"Oh there you are dear! I've looked all over for you and Bret said he had gotten you settled. I tell you, I am just exhausted already. I just couldn't wait to come and see what you think of your rooms. I decorated them for you. I mean, I didn't do a lot because I figured you would want to make them your own but I wanted you to have everything waiting for you. What do you think?"

Addy was confused. How long had her mother known that they would be moving here?

"It's very nice Mom. Thank you but did you know that someone left their clothes in the closet? I think they're all new."

Joanie laughed loudly and said, "Of course they're new! They're *yours* silly goose. I bought them for you. I thought it would be the perfect start to your new life. Now you have a new wardrobe as well."

"They look really expensive Mom. When did you find time to do all this?"

"Oh don't you worry about that. It's all good things from here on out baby. Trust me on that one," she said with a wink at her daughter and headed out the door leaving Addy confused and a bit bewildered by all that had taken place in such a short time.

Whose money had bought all these nice clothes and furnishings? They were completely out of cash weren't they? Did Bret's money buy all of these things? She would unpack then have a talk with her new mommy. There were a lot of details that she wanted to hear and she refused to put it off another day.

Chapter 18

The unpacking process took a few hours to complete. When the boxes were empty and Addy had showered to wash the dust and grime off, she went in search of her mother. Having no luck downstairs she went out into the yard to have a look around. She noticed a back exit just off from the kitchen. It seemed to lead through a laundry area that was, in keeping with the rest of the house, quite large. There were two industrial washers and dryers standing poised for duty as if twenty people lived in the house.

She exited through the door and down the steps onto a paved breezeway. It took her out to a gate that opened up into the pool area. It was the biggest swimming pool she had ever seen complete with a diving board and a huge slide. A party-sized hot tub sat adjacent to the main pool. There was even a small cabana off to one side with an outdoor shower area attached. Striped lounge chairs dotted the sidewalks along the pool. It looked like a hotel pool she thought.

"Going for a swim so soon?"

Addy jumped like she had been pinched.

"You scared the life out of me! Do you always sneak up on people like that?"

"Only when I think it may scare them," he said shrugging his shoulders.

"You're terrible, you know that right? I was looking for my mom. I need to talk to her. Do you know where she went?"

Bret looked up in the direction of the second floor and pointed.

"She said she was too tired to go on today and she was going to lie down in one of the guest rooms so she wouldn't be disturbed."

He could see the frustration on her face and asked, "Is something wrong? Is it your room? Are you hungry? Can I help with anything?"

She stepped back from him and waved her hands.

"I'm not a toddler. You don't have to ask me if I'm cold, or hungry or got a boo boo. I just needed to ask some questions, that's all."

She had offended him or at the very least, hurt his feelings. He had been trying to help and what did she do? She cut him down sarcastically.

"I'm sorry Bret. I didn't mean to snap. I'm just tired and irritated. It isn't your fault. Maybe you could be of some help. I'm just wondering how my mom had the time to do all this decorating and shopping between work and classes."

Bret tilted his head and knitted his brows together. Oh no. Joanie hadn't told Addy anything. How long did she plan to keep this girl in the dark, he wondered.

She could see on his face that he knew more than he had told her about this speedy marriage and relocation.

"Is there something I should know Bret?"

This was the definition of trapped between a rock and a hard place. Was he supposed to tell her? Didn't she have a right to know? Sadly there was no time to

85

consider these things. She was asking a question and if he chose to lie, it could ruin any future trust between them.

"Addy, I'm sure your mom was planning on telling you everything when everyone was settled. Why don't you wait and when she gets up we can all sit down and talk."

That sounded reasonable to him. It did *not* sound reasonable to her.

"Wait? That's all I do is wait! I wait for her to talk to me and to comfort me. I wait for her to tell me she's married or that we've lost our house. Hell, I even wait for her to know I still exist! I want to know things and she won't tell me so if you aren't going to tell me either, we have nothing more to say to one another."

She darted around Bret and headed for the breezeway. Her hair was fanning out behind her like fire in the sunlight. Bret ran to catch her and managed to grab her arm before she disappeared in the house.

"Wait. Just calm down and we will talk. I'll do my best to answer your questions but please know that you're putting me in an awful position with your mom. This is her place to talk about these things with you."

He motioned in the direction of a patio table and chairs, silently suggesting that she sit down. With no words, she did just that. Bret sat down in the chair beside her and scrubbed his face hard on the palms of his hands.

"Okay, let's have it. Fire away with your questions."

Finally someone was willing to shed some light on her gray and chaotic world.

"I want to know how Mom had time to prepare all of this for us. I want to know when you got married and why nobody told me it was happening. Has anyone told our other family about this? Do your parents even know?"

He had thought one question would come and then maybe a discussion but she was firing them as fast as her brain could think them up.

"Wow. You gave this a lot more thought than I expected. Okay, let's see if I can tackle these for you. First, your mom has time now because she doesn't work or go to school anymore. She quit both of those over two months ago right after we married and nobody told you because she said you couldn't handle the shock. She said you were too emotional and it would only hurt you; better for us to wait. I don't think she has told anyone else in your family but yes, my parents do know however they haven't met Joanie yet."

Two months. Her mother had been married for two whole months and had hid it from her. She didn't know how to respond. Too emotional? She was being blamed for being too emotional? She almost laughed out loud but when her mouth opened, nothing came out.

"Are you okay Addy? You asked, I told you. Isn't that what you wanted?"

Bret didn't know if he had made a huge mistake or not by having this talk. Her silence was making his stomach churn.

"No. I'm fine. You are being honest and I appreciate it. I'm just shocked. I also realize you were right. I do need to speak to my mother about this. If you will excuse me I need to go prepare myself for school. We start back in a day or two and I have to be ready."

She didn't make eye contact as she got out of her chair and retreated into the house.

What had he done? Would his new wife be very happy with him when she found out her daughter knew it all? Probably not, he decided. He would cross that bridge when he came to it. He could always blame it on the fact that he was new to this marriage thing and wasn't schooled on how to handle a step-daughter who wasn't far from his own age. This was all turning out to be more complex than he imagined.

Chapter 19

It turned out to be three full days before Addy got an opportunity to talk to her mother or even see her again after the day of the move. She had returned to school and was grateful for the comfort of Drew. They were settling into more of a comfortable boyfriend and girlfriend relationship. It seemed that after everything that she had been through the only good so far was that it had brought her and Drew closer.

She had forsaken all her old friends completely and was spending all her free time with him. He was her rock, her sounding board and her best friend. They made a standing date for her to go with him and his family to church each Sunday as well as dinner with them once a week. She was eager to bring Drew to her new home and enjoy the pool and the surrounding beauty before it was swallowed up by the cool winds of the fall weather but she didn't want to do it until she knew where things stood with her mom.

Addy happened to be coming home from Drew's house one night when she ran head on into her mother crossing the foyer.

"Mother, can we talk for a minute?" she asked quickly.

"*Mother*? Why don't you call me 'mom' anymore? Mother sounds so formal. It also sounds like something you would call your mother-in-law." She laughed at her own joke.

"Sorry mom. So, can we talk?"

Joanie waved her daughter into the sitting room and seated herself in the high back chair. Addy noticed her mom seemed to sit straighter and crossed her legs as if she were attending a tea party. She looked to be wearing some type of dressy pant suit as well. It was not Joanie's normal style at all. Her mom was always beautiful and of course looked professional when she went to work but this was on a different level. This was odd.

"Am I interrupting your plans to go somewhere Mom? You look dressed up."

Joanie scowled darkly and answered, "No I'm not going anywhere. Can't I look presentable at home without having to go somewhere?"

"Yes Moth...I mean Mom. I'm sorry. I just wanted you to know that Bret and I talked and I know everything."

Joanie's eyes grew large and wide. Surely he had not told her literally everything. Her new young husband wouldn't betray her that way.

"He told me that you guys have been married for almost two months and that you don't work or go to school anymore."

There seemed to be a mental exhale on Joanie's behalf. He had not told her anything more than the basics. He was smarter than that.

"I just want you to know mom that I'm not happy about being kept in the dark and I hope that in the future you will treat me with more respect and be honest."

A sudden smile spread across Joanie's face as she cooed "Certainly honey. I promise it won't happen again. Now that our little talk is over I'm going upstairs to compare color samples. I'm thinking of doing some redecorating."

Addy had her say and felt a bit better but it seemed like her mother heard her but didn't care. She dismissed her by leaving the room without another word. It looked like this new life would be much more different than she thought, only in ways she didn't expect.

As the warmer weather started moving out of the way for the leaves to change colors, Addy's seventeenth birthday was approaching fast. Her mom and dad had always made a big deal out her birthday. They would throw her a big party with all her friends. The only thing that changed over the years was the maturity of the entertainment. She no longer had clowns at her parties when she turned twelve. Her request to omit them was met with sadness from her father.

"My little punkin is growing up. Okay, no clowns at the party except for me," he had joked. She remembered her last birthday which seemed like a lifetime ago instead of a mere eleven months and two weeks. Her dad had sent her roses at school along with a bouquet of colorful 'Happy Birthday' balloons. She received sixteen roses, one for each year of her life. When she arrived home she had a beautiful necklace on her bed with a heart shaped pendant along with a note telling her to dress nice and be ready in an hour.

Her parents had driven her into the neighboring town to a very upscale restaurant where many of her closest friends were waiting to celebrate with her. It was such a happy night and her parents seemed so perfect together.

How had she totally missed what was going on behind the curtain? Looking back she felt like such a fool.

How could she get through her birthday this year without her daddy here to help her celebrate? She couldn't imagine it. So far her mother had not said one word about her birthday so Addy was certain there was an epic surprise. Her mother was not one to overlook a reason to decorate and plan. Drew had already gotten her a gift because his family would be out of town on her birthday visiting his grandmother in Tennessee. She was ailing and they would be going to spend some much needed time with her and their extended family. After church service the week before her birthday, the two of them were standing in the vestibule talking with some of the other young people, laughing and joking when Drew pulled a small box out of his jacket pocket. The other teens smiled knowingly and quickly excused themselves to give them privacy.

"I feel so bad that we have to be apart on your birthday, especially your first one without your dad, but I wanted to go ahead and give you your gift," he said, stretching out his arm and extending the box to her. It was a small dark blue velvet box with a gold ribbon on it.

"Oh Drew, you didn't have to do that," she exclaimed even though she was eager and excited to open the tiny box.

"Yes I did. You're the best girl any guy could ask for and I wanted you to know how special you are, on your special day, and every day after that."

She grinned and hastily untied the ribbon. Inside the box was a small gold band with an inscription. The words ran circular around following the band. It said 'I Promise. Love Drew.' Before she could ask what it was that he was promising, he said, "It's a promise ring. It means that I promise to love you now and from here on out. I know we still have another year of school but I want my intentions known. I love you and I hope you love me

91

which means that I pray that one day you and I can have a real future. But until then, I promise I'm yours if you will be mine."

He had practiced that speech over and over the night before. He was so nervous. Neither of them had used the term love yet and he was really hoping he wasn't way off the mark. When he looked into her eyes he could see the pools of water collecting in the corners. As one spilled out, she wiped it away and looked up at him.

"That's the most beautiful thing anyone has ever said to me. I love you too Drew and I promise that I'm yours forever if we are lucky."

She threw her arms around him and for the first time in so long she felt like one of the luckiest girls in the world. Her father would have loved Drew and she was sure he would be pleased with their relationship. She couldn't ask for more.

Chapter 20

The morning of her birthday was a Saturday and Addy had woken up feeling a tingle of anticipation. Her mother had still not let anything about her birthday slip so she must be planning something far more extravagant than ever. It made her feel like a small child again. She planned to attack her first day of being seventeen with an unusual vigor she hadn't known in over a year.

Addy jumped out of bed, showered and changed into a nice pair of jeans with a burnt orange long sleeved top. All shades of orange looked good on her because it made her hair color glow. She topped this off with her leather topsider shoes and she was off to breakfast.

Since moving in she had hardly seen Bret due to his constant work schedule. It seemed that he was a workaholic. It made her wonder how he and her mother ever spent any time together. He was always working or gone and Joanie was always gone or locked in the bedroom resting alone. Her mother had even talked him into hiring a cook that came in six days a week and a maid to come in every three days. It was as if she were busier now than she had been when she worked, cooked, cleaned, and took care of her young daughter. She imagined that Bret was bending over backwards to impress and spoil his new wife. He could afford it so she guessed there was no harm.

This particular morning however, Bret was seated at the breakfast table when she entered the room. She was surprised to see him but it was nice to know she wouldn't be eating alone for a change. Their new cook was a woman who was in her sixties named Margie. Margie was a sweet lady who seemed quite passionate about cooking and she was quite wonderful at her job. Addy was actually worried she would grow fat eating Margie's delicious concoctions all the time. Her birthday breakfast was going to be blueberry crepes, sausage links, fresh fruit and scrambled eggs.

Yummy!

Being in the great mood she was, it took a minute for her to realize that Bret had not acknowledged her arrival. Her mother must have him on a strict hush policy about any birthday plans because he had also been quiet about it.

"Good morning Bret," she cheerfully sang as she seated herself at the breakfast table. He looked up through squinted eyes, holding his fork loosely. His eyes were a little puffy and his hair looked disheveled. He didn't look like a man who had slept at all the night before. Dark shadows smeared the underneath of his eyes.

"Are you alright? Did you not sleep well last night or did mom keep you up discussing the never ending redecorating she plans to devote her life to?" she asked while spearing a sausage link to put on her plate.

"No, nothing like that. You have to actually talk to someone to keep them awake. You have to actually be in the same room to keep them awake, I should say," he grumbled.

This puzzled her. She was not aware that Joanie and her new man were having problems so soon. She forked a bite of crepe into her mouth and asked, "Are you and Mom fighting or something?" Talking with her mouth full made it come out something like, "Ah woo a moh fightin a sumpin?"

"Fighting? No. Your mom has decided she doesn't have enough personal space so she has relocated to the suite down the hall from mine with the sitting room like yours. When I offered to move my things as well she informed me that she would be the only one sleeping in that room. It seems I have been restricted to my bedroom while she has her own."

He had begun angrily stabbing his eggs like they were attempting to escape and he had to catch them or lose them. Addy didn't know how to respond. Her mother and father had always shared a bedroom even when they fought. The idea of newlyweds who sleep apart sounded silly to her and obviously it was downright abhorrent to Bret. She couldn't blame him. What twenty-five year old guy wanted to get married to sleep alone? Surely this phase would pass; once her mom got used to their new life, she would go back to normal.

Bret looked up suddenly as if he just realized who he was talking to.

"I'm sorry Addy. I shouldn't be telling you this stuff. Don't worry, I'm fine. Your mom is fine. Just forget I said anything."

"It's okay, really. You don't have to apologize to me. I just hope this doesn't put a damper on anything that you guys have planned for my birthday today. I want everyone to be as happy as I am. I've got a good feeling about today."

She noticed that Bret was staring at her with the strangest expression. Finally he said, "It's your birthday today? I haven't heard anything about it." He was going

95

to carry this to the bitter end and he was playing dumb very well.

"It's okay. I know you probably have been warned not to leak a single word of her plans to me. I won't get you in trouble."

Bret was shaking his head with a true look of confusion on his face.

"Addy, I'm serious. I don't know what you are talking about. Joanie has said absolutely nothing about your birthday to me. When I came down this morning Margie told me that Joanie had asked her to tell me she wouldn't be home today or tonight. She has plans to drive into Atlanta with a girlfriend of hers, shop and spend the night. That's why I was so mad. She moved out of our bedroom last night and didn't even bother to stick around and talk it out with me today."

The air suddenly felt like someone had sucked it out of the room with a giant vacuum. She couldn't reconcile that her mother had ignored her birthday. How could this happen? She wanted to think this was part of their ruse but the haggard look on Bret's face showed that he was completely serious. She didn't know whether to cry or break a plate. Crying won out. She began to sob right there at the breakfast table, loudly.

Bret jumped up and came around to her side of the table. He pulled her to him and let her have her cry. His new wife should be ashamed of herself. This girl had been through too much to be treated this way. Joanie had shown him how sweet and loving she was in the beginning. He thought she was the total package. She was mature, hardworking, tender, a devoted parent, smart and very beautiful in a natural way. He was besotted in no time. He just couldn't believe that her husband took such a jewel for granted. Now he was beginning to think it wasn't a jewel he had found but instead it was fool's gold.

Joanie McMullen may have been those things but Joanie Thomas was selfish, self-centered, flippant, lazy, cold and vain. Gone were the days of pulling her long hair into a pony tail to go for a walk in the woods. Now her hair had to be styled to perfection, makeup expertly applied and her designer clothes had to be fashion photo ready just to emerge from her room on a normal day.

The worst was the naps. She seemed to exhaust herself simply by taking a telephone call. Anytime Bret suggested they do something together it was always the same excuse day or night. She was too tired. She needed a nap. This marriage was becoming a nightmare for him and he could see that Addy was a fellow inmate in this prison of Joanie's emotions with him, to no fault of her own.

When she stopped her wailing, Bret turned her face up to his and said, "Go wash your face and meet me in the foyer in twenty minutes."

"Why? I just want to go to my room," she whimpered.

"No ma'am, not today. This is your special day and damn it, you and I are going to celebrate. I say to heck with your mother; it's her loss."

Before she could object again, he released her and headed out of the room. Her heart was broken that she had been discarded and forgotten by the only parent she had left. It just didn't make sense to her. Mothers were supposed to love their children more than their own life, right? At that moment, Addy thought someone should have told her mom that fact because she obviously didn't know.

Chapter 21

It had taken almost the entire twenty minutes for the puffy red swelling around her eyes to go down as well as the involuntary sniffles from her outburst. She felt somewhat childish now that she had calmed down. She was seventeen and she couldn't expect everyone to treat her like a little girl anymore. Her mother had been through as much as she had in this past year and she could exercise a little understanding for her considering the change in Joanie recently. She consoled herself by thinking that when her mom realized the date, she would most definitely scramble to call her only child on her special day. Until that time, she would cheer back up and see what Bret had in store for her day.

True to his word, Bret was standing in the foyer in twenty-two minutes; showered, shaved and looking very handsome in his jeans, green polo shirt and sneakers. A nice ball cap adorned the top of his head as well. She had never seen him dress so casual before. It made him look very much like a teenager. The two of them could have been mistaken easily for boyfriend and girlfriend instead of step-daughter and step-father.

Addy hadn't really felt how unconventional the scenario was until now. How could her mother feel comfortable with someone so young? It was still very strange to think about. It really was nice of him to try and save the day. She felt badly for him as well. He was just a young guy who bit off more than he could chew and now he was struggling to play his part. It was a sweet gesture and it didn't go unappreciated. With no family visiting anymore and no friends except her boyfriend who was out of town, it would have been a lonely day if Bret had not intervened.

The day began by going to the large indoor mall located about one hour away from their town. The mall boasted to be the largest indoor outlet mall in the southeast. The two of them started at the four thousand square foot arcade and by the time they had finished, Addy was sure they had played every game on the floor. Bret had even team raced with her on the virtual dirt bikes. She had laughed until she almost fell off her defacto bike, when he wrecked repeatedly. She had to admit that she couldn't remember when she had had this much fun.

The game playing ceased when both parties agreed that they were starving. Their crepes had worn off somewhere around the racecar simulator.

"Poor Margie," Bret said. "What will she do with nobody to cook lunch for? I bet she starts baking or something like that. The woman is a cooking addict."

Addy bent over giggling. "Yes, that she is but I love her cooking so let's not get her help for that addiction."

They high fived each other in mutual approval.

Bret thought about how long it had been since he had just went out and enjoyed himself with free abandon and realized it had been quite a while. It was possibly his sophomore year of college and if he recalled correctly, it involved a large keg of beer. Not long after that, his father's words of wisdom came crashing in and he buckled down. It was studying day and night. There were dates but nothing too serious or too long. The dates he had gone on with Joanie were always grown up dates; dates to impress. They weren't the fun carefree impulsive dates like this, he thought. Catching his roaming mind instantly he chastised himself mentally. 'This is not a date you moron. This is your wife's daughter, nothing more.' It had to be a momentary lapse of the here and now, didn't it? The girl he had been spending the day with didn't resemble the woman he married in anyway at all. The sad part of it all was that his wife was the complimenting partner.

Lunch was agreed on at a sports bar that just happened to be showing college football. He had offered a swanky restaurant but Addy had declined. She said it would put a damper on the fun they were having if she had to act stuck up just to have lunch. She also made a comment about how she refused to be persuaded to eat snails.

"I have never eaten snails, thank you very much," Bret spouted with feigned offense.

"Sure you haven't. All rich people eat snails. It's okay snail eater, I won't hold it against you."

Bret flipped her ear and she squealed.

After lunch they decided on an outdoor concert that was hosting several indie bands both of them had heard of once or twice. The day had been amazing and Addy had been a ball of infectious energy the entire time. Bret was almost sad to see it end. Real life seemed suddenly so dull compared to this.

Driving on their way home, Addy was sitting in the passenger side singing along to the radio. They reached a four way stop about five miles from home, which happened to be totally empty and dark at 11:22 p.m. and before he could accelerate, Addy turned to him.

"Thank you for making this the best birthday I have ever had. It was almost the worst birthday and you turned it all around. Thank you so much," she gushed.

Before he could answer she leaned across the car and threw her arms around his neck in gratitude. Neither of them could have imagined what it would do to feel one another so closely.

As soon as she had reacted, she knew it was a mistake but it was too late. Her arms were already around him and his scent had filled her nostrils. It was strong and deep like a warm summer night. Her fingertips on her right hand were brushing the tips of his dark hair. She was locked and didn't know what to do next.

Bret was in much the same predicament. That beautiful hair that was fire red in the sun of the day was a deep velvet red in the night and he could smell the scent of jasmine as it lay along the side of his face. Her shampoo must be what he smelled, he tried to rationalize. The tenderness of her touch was so much more than he had experienced with his wife even when they were in the dating phase.

"You're welcome. I had a great time too," he choked out as she began to slowly release him. His foot continued to be glued to the brake as they sat at the stop sign. Addy leaned back to her side of the car and Bret accelerated. They didn't speak again throughout the ride home. Thank God the radio still played to quell the awkward silence that had engulfed them.

When Bret had parked, they took no extra time exiting the car. You would have thought the interior was smoldering and about to flame up by the way each one jumped out and headed for the door.

Entering the foyer, Addy immediately noticed something different. It was a scent. She turned to see her mother striding towards her.

"Adelicia, happy birthday darling! I'm such a nit wit. I got settled into my suite in Atlanta and made it all the way to dinner at the restaurant when my friend Jill mentioned today's date and I instantly arranged to drive home. I do hope you can forgive me sweetheart."

Still very shaken from the awkward embrace she had shared with Bret, Addy was grateful for an extra person to settle the tension even if it was the strange new version of her mother.

"Of course Mom. I understand." She hugged her mother lightly. She always appeared to be a fragile vase these days. Addy avoided physical contact for fear of breaking her in some way or even worse, smudging her makeup.

"So where have you two been tonight? Did you throw a party without me?"

Joanie looked from her daughter to her husband and back again, waiting for one of them to answer her.

"Bret took me to an outdoor concert for my birthday and it ran late. We're just getting in," Addy explained quickly. There was no mention of the entire day that had been theirs to enjoy.

Joanie looked on her husband as you would a dog that had just fetched your favorite slippers and said, "Thank you dear. My little life saver." She walked past Bret with nothing more than a pat on the shoulder as if he were the butler taking her coat.

"Come dear, I want to show you what I brought you for your birthday. I just know you're going to love it all." Joanie was excitedly motioning for Addy to follow her. Bret was standing stock still and his face had turned a deep shade of red that almost bordered on purple. She hadn't noticed it before but it seemed her mother's behavior towards Bret had become condescending and authoritative. She was even speaking to Addy differently. The old Mom she knew would never have called her darling. It sounded silly just to hear it come out like 'daaahling'.

Thinking it best to follow her mother before Bret exploded, she darted past him and followed Joanie up the stairs. When Addy entered her mother's new bedroom it was like entering a dressing room assigned to movie star. The walls hung with elaborate paintings and shopping bags littered the sitting room furniture that appeared to be of an antique nature. Her mother was standing above a huge pile of purchases, digging through them as a dog would dig for a bone. Every other garment was discarded to a different pile until she popped up with an armload of items. Dumping them on the end table beside her daughter she encouraged Addy to look at what she had brought.

"Go on dear. See what you think. I know I forgot your day but I'm forever thinking of you while I'm on holiday."

There were many nice outfits in the pile as well as a soft leather riding jacket and kid gloves. The clothing was lovely but not very practical. She wondered where she would ever wear some of these things. Her mom's insane behavior and new tastes were becoming such a curiosity that Addy couldn't contain it any longer.

"Did you just say 'when you're on holiday'?" What are you British now? What's with all the darlings and dears and the stuffy pant suits and the compulsive shopping? I really have to know, is my mother still in there somewhere at all? I feel like I'm living with one of the Gabor sisters."

She hadn't intended to spew all her feelings out but once that faucet was opened, there was no going back. The look that her mother gave her could only be described as icy. A garment bag that had been hanging on her wrist fell to the floor and within seconds Joanie was in her daughter's face.

"Let me tell you something you ungrateful brat. Your father promised me the world when he married me and what did I get? I got an absent husband, a crummy job at the phone company and mismatched furniture. That's what I got! I busted my hump to take you to events and practices and parties with no thanks from anyone. Now I have a man who can give me the things I deserve and I won't let you talk down to me for it. Do you hear me? You can speak to me with some respect or do not speak to me at all. I will not apologize to you for acting like I have class."

Addy was flabbergasted. Had she really just said those things while waving her finger in the face of her only child? Had she gone mad? Who was this woman in front of her? Addy's red-haired Irish McMullen blood had begun to boil and something told her she had now officially been pushed to the brink of no return.

"How dare you talk about my father that way! Our life was good! If you didn't like us you should have left long ago and by the way, no amount of money will buy class for some people so stop shopping for it!"

Joanie swung with one fluid motion and slapped her daughter hard across the face. It was the first time she had ever struck Addy and the shock rippled through her like a tidal wave.

"Let that be your first lesson Adelicia. Never speak to me like that again. I want you out of my room and I don't want to see your face until you can apologize for disrespecting me. Get out!"

A gust of wind could not have fled her mother's room quicker; out she blew with her hand holding the stinging mark across her left cheek. As she exited the door she almost knocked Bret down. She didn't even give him a chance to stop her.

Bret didn't need to see the evidence; he knew why she was holding her face. He had heard the slap from the stairway and rushed to see what happened. Only he got there too late. This woman he was married to had become a monster right before his eyes.

He was standing in the doorway watching her pick up the discarded gifts and place them back into the bags. When she realized he was there she smiled like nothing bad had ever happened.

"Bret darling. I missed you terribly. Thank you for taking my pouting child to celebrate her birthday. I know it must have made for a boring evening. You sacrifice so much for us."

Her tidbits of praise would not work tonight. Bret was angry.

"Save your pathetic babbling for someone else Joanie. You had no right to hit her. You're the one who forgot her birthday. You're the one who's acting like a freak these days. Hell, you're the one who moved out of our bedroom while we're still newlyweds. What's that all about?"

He was torn between rushing out to check on Addy or jumping across the pile of wasted merchandise on the floor and choking the wench to death. His anger was brewing hot so he was really leaning towards the latter choice.

"What I do with her is none of your business so I thank you to stay out of it. I won't have you babying her like her father did. She needs to be tougher. As for my bedroom, that isn't your concern either. Don't worry, I will still do my wifely duties when I need to but until then, I can't have you draining the life out of me with your endless groping and pestering. Be a grown up and learn some restraint please. Now go away, I'm tired. I need my rest."

If he had stayed any longer he knew that he would have committed an act he would regret for the rest of his life so he backed out of the room and headed down the corridor. He knocked on Addy's door but there was no answer.

"Addy, it's me. Can I come in? I just want to make sure you're okay. Please answer me."

After a couple minutes of waiting patiently by a silent door, she cracked it open and answered him. "I'm fine. Please just go to bed and don't worry about me."

He pushed open the door to get a better view of her face. There it was streaked scarlet in a vertical stain. It was a handprint and it belonged to her mother. She had been crying again. He could tell.

Chapter 22

Bret gently pushed open the outer door and Addy didn't resist. Once the door closed she crumpled on the sofa and cried softly into the arm rest. Bret sat down with her and tried to hold her while she cried. Having done this very thing one time today already, he was becoming a pro at it. He just wished that life would give this girl a break. He could use one himself right about now. Life had always dealt him a pretty good hand but it seemed like the tables were turning for him since his recent nuptials.

His father had warned him not to rush into a marriage with an older woman until he could get to know her better. He also warned him to make her sign a prenuptial agreement. Did he listen to either warning? No, he did not.

Now he lived with Satan's Queen and if he tried to divorce her, he had no doubt she would retaliate with an expensive attorney, on his dime. She would plead the poor widow who was taken advantage of by the young playboy and threw out on the streets after she lost her home and her job. He could see the headline now: Woman takes HALF. The thought made him sick. His current concern however was not his money but this abused and hurting young woman in front of him. His heart ached to stop her pain. His parents had been loving and his mother devoted to their family but he had friends in school who weren't so lucky. He had seen what selfish uncaring parents put their kids through and it was a sad shame.

Bret began smoothing back her hair from her tear stained face. It had grown longer in the past few months and it waved much like her mothers. He couldn't stop himself from touching it over and over again. It was soft and for some reason it seemed like a gesture that one person would do to comfort another. His own mother was forever smoothing back his hair when he was a child who had fallen off his bike or scraped up his knees. He was trying to dig into the only well of resources he had at his age. Those resources would have to come from his own childhood since he had no kids of his own yet.

Call it lack of tenderness or just plain insanity but Addy was so starved for any human connection that she began to respond in a much unexpected way. She turned to look at him and found him staring at her with his heart in his eyes. That dark stare was so open and sad that she couldn't tear her gaze away from his. How long had it been since someone had looked at her with such deep feeling? She suddenly couldn't recall. Time felt suspended and sadness was all she could experience. The desire to stop that bottomless pit of grief was overwhelming. Within seconds the two faces were coming together and their lips met. She could feel his warm breath under her nose. His hands buried deep in her hair to run down her neck.

All thoughts seemed to disappear. Addy could hear his breath and feel his pulse pressing in on her. His smell was as intoxicating as his dark eyes. It was so wonderful to feel a loving touch again. So great to connect with someone who hadn't abandoned her. The moment swept them both up into a frenzy and before either of them could stop themselves or realize what it was they were about to do, it was too late. They had traveled past the point of going back.

The sofa in her sitting room had witnessed her very first act of lovemaking and to her sudden realization, it had not been with her boyfriend but with the person who was supposed to be her step-father. Alarm bells were ringing in her ears.

What had they done? She kept playing it in her mind even while she and Bret lay partially clothed holding one another. It was a fact. She had wanted him and he had wanted her. Correction, they had *needed* one another. She had enjoyed herself but she wasn't sure what happens next. Neither she nor Bret was sure about anything other than the fact that they had made the situation a million times worse than it had been when he knocked on her door an hour ago.

Both of them had redressed and without much discussion Bret told her he was going to his room so she could rest and have her privacy. Once he was gone she went into her bathroom to change into her pajamas. Looking in the mirror she could see that the red hand print on her face had almost disappeared but the red hand prints on the rest of her body told the tale of the forbidden act she had just engaged in. Her body and mind was her enemy because one felt guilty and the other felt fulfilled. Which one was right? She knew the answer to that question and it only made her guilt worse.

What would Drew think of her? He would leave her. What would God think of her? He would find her to be a sinner. She was unworthy to know him anymore. What was she going to do?

She had to think of something because Drew would be back in a few days and, well, God was there now according to the Sunday School lessons she had been sitting in on so avoiding him was useless. God just got a front row seat to her whoredom. Then of course, morning had to come and she had to face Bret as well as her hateful mother. Would Bret regret what happened? Part of her hoped he would and that they could pretend it didn't happen. The other part of her hoped he didn't because she had wanted to be loved and he gave that feeling to her, even if it was only a facade.

Chapter 23

Facing everyone did not come as quickly as she had assumed it would. Her mother was upholding her cruel words by making sure she did not see her daughter's face until she made the first attempt to apologize for her behavior. Addy could not even imagine how her mom would react when she found out that her daughter had more to ask forgiveness for than just speaking her mind. No matter how mean Joanie was to her, she knew that what she had done was unacceptable and her mom didn't deserve it. Addy had not been raised to behave in such a way. Her father would be ashamed of her.

The thought made her want to cry again. How she missed her father. She could talk to him about anything and he always helped steer her in the right direction. How would her dad steer her right now? She tried hard to conjure words that she felt he would say and all she kept coming back to was: Be Honest. She could hear her father telling her to be honest with her mother and with Drew and face the consequences but could she really risk doing that? She had already lost so much in her life, could she lose the two of them also?

Bret had thrown himself into his work for two days. Margie had even been bringing his meals to his office trying to encourage him to open a few windows to let some light into the room.

"Nobody wants to eat in a dark and gloomy office dear. Let the light shine," Margie kept telling him.

"Thanks Margie but I'm crunching to meet a deadline. Thank you for worrying about me though," he smiled and replied.

"It's no problem lovey. Someone around here has to look after you and Addy. Lord knows no one else will."

Margie covered her mouth in a fast effort to catch her words before they came out but it was too late. She had said what she had been thinking.

"Bret honey I meant no disrespect to your wife. I was just meaning...."

Bret held his hand up to stop her from finishing her sentence.

"It's okay, really. I know what you meant and from the bottom of my heart I agree with you. Your attention and devotion to us is more appreciated than you know."

The lady nodded and softly backed out of the room so as not to further the awkward moment.

So, even the cook knows his wife is a vapid shell of a human, he thought. He felt like a fool. Everyone could see it but him until it had hit him right in the jaw. Now he had gone and fallen for his own step-daughter. The ugly truth was that his marriage to her mother was disgusting him. What had he been thinking getting together with a woman so much older than him? He wished he had listened to his dad. Where did that leave him now?

Margie was right. He had to get out of this office for a while and get some fresh air, clear his mind. Staying locked away was driving him crazy.

His wife had made no attempt to see him, talk to him or even call him since their encounter several days earlier. She had his money; obviously she didn't need him as well. One lover would do and right now she was entertaining his bank account. The thought made him angry.

Leaving his office, he grabbed a light jacket because the weather was unseasonably warm but the wind was blowing sharply. He wanted to walk down to the pond and just watch the birds and the geese that made their winter home there. Nature had always been a natural healer of the mind for him.

Exiting through the rear of the house Bret made his way towards the northeast end of the property at the wooded tree line. He continued on a well-trodden foot path that his family and their cattle had used for years to reach the pond. The path wasn't as easy to see this time of year due to all the leaves fallen on the ground but he could have followed it in the dark with his eyes closed; he knew it that well.

Taking his time ambling through the brush and stopping to inspect evidence of local animals, he was beginning to feel much of the stress slip off his shoulders. This had been a good idea he decided. When the thick brush broke way to a clearing, he pushed his way through to the banks of the pond. It was a lovely sight to behold but not near as beautiful as the girl sitting bundled up on its shores.

Addy was sitting on a blanket with another blanket wrapped around her shoulders. Her flaming hair was down and she had a stocking cap over her skull. The light caught every strand and caused it to reflect like a halo around her face. She must have been in such deep thought she didn't even hear him approach. He was glad. He could use this moment to look at her unfiltered; see her in a way he normally didn't get to experience. The melancholy look on her face tore at his heart. This was his fault. He had done this to her. Her life was

113

complicated enough and here he was throwing a wrench even further into it. He knew it had been selfish but once they had touched in that way, he had been unable to stop. The whole day they had spent together was so fresh and Joanie's rejection was still sitting on the surface too. It just made a heady concoction that made their alliance inevitable. The fact remained that he was the older of the two and was more experienced than she was. He should have been the one to make the right decision and stop. Better yet, he should have seen it for what it was becoming and never followed her to her room for the purpose of comforting her to begin with. Yes, it was his fault. Addy could not be blamed.

His shoe snapped a small twig in half as he shifted his weight. The sound cracked in the air loud enough for her to realize she wasn't alone. Addy turned to find Bret standing about twenty yards away just at the edge of the clearing watching her. The sight of his face after several days of agony felt like a breeze of cool air on a hot day. She had been nervous to confront him but she couldn't deny that his touch was the dominant thought of her every waking hour.

He truly was handsome. The expression on his face was much like a little boy who waited to see if he would be punished for knocking over a glass. She could tell that their entanglement had affected him as strongly as it had her. There was a moment that she almost expected him to dart back into the woods like a frightened deer but instead, he slowly walked towards the water's edge where she sat.

"May I join you?"

"Sure. It looks like my date has abandoned me anyway. You come here often?"

He chuckled under his breath. She could still make a joke, which was good. Maybe she didn't hate him as much as he thought she would.

She continued to look out across the water as he lowered himself down on the blanket beside her. No one spoke for several minutes. Only the sounds of the birds twittering and the squirrels rustling through the trees could be heard. Finally Bret broke the ice.

"Whatcha thinking about?"

Wow. Had he really just said that? He felt like the world's biggest moron. Did he think that she was thinking of something other than the two of them naked on her sitting room sofa? Dear Lord, how stupid could he be?

She didn't seem to take offense at his question.

"I'm thinking of Drew. He'll be home tonight and he wants me to visit him. I don't know what to do. I feel like he will look at me and see the words written on my face. I look at the ring he gave me and feel like dirt. The problem is that I'm not sure if I'm trying to decide how to tell him or how to lie to him. Does that make me a horrible person?"

He knew that how he answered that question could go a long way towards containing this situation or causing the main explosion. He knew that at the moment he was the only person in the world that she could be completely candid with. The same went for her. Bret could not open up to anyone else about this so he might as well exercise blunt honesty and see where it took him.

"I can't answer that. You and I are in the same boat. If we tell, your mother will leave me, take my money and turn on you. If we keep quiet, you and I have to learn to live with what we did. We just have to figure out how to live like it never happened."

That sounded so logical. Funny how logic never seems to find a place in decisions of the heart though. It was easy to say what had to be done but much harder to actually do it. The absence of truth for the past year of her life had caused Addy to need it now more than ever.

"What do you feel for me Bret? Honestly, no bull."

She turned her gaze from the water to stare into his eyes like she was waiting for the truth to pop up on a teleprompter.

"I don't know exactly."

She exhaled loudly and turned back to the water.

"Don't do that. You're not being fair. I do love your mother or at least I thought I loved your mother until she turned into this thing she is now but I know that's no excuse. I've grown to love you too but I never have been able to think of you as my step-kid. I've tried. Then when I saw her tear you down and we spent the day together, you were everything that I thought she was when I met her. You made me feel alive and fun, interesting and free. I just got caught up in it all. Then later when we, when we were in your room, it was like you were a magnet and I was a lump of metal. I know that sounds dumb but I'm a guy and this stuff is hard for me to explain. What more do you want me to say?"

Nothing really, she thought. He had done a fine job of throwing it all on the table and he was right, it wasn't fair to put it all on him. He couldn't know what to do any more than she did.

"What do you feel for me?" he asked in return. "I shouldn't be the only one to have to answer that question Addy."

Again, he was right. She had opened that door and now she had to participate as well.

"I care for you very much. You've been my only ally in this house since my whole world was turned upside down. You became my friend when you didn't have to. I won't lie and say that I don't find everything about you attractive. I really do. I also won't say that you took advantage of me because you didn't. I wanted what happened as much as you did but in the light of day I knew there was no hope. I'm going to ask God for forgiveness and hope that our secret never comes out. That's all I can do, isn't it?"

She was much older than her seventeen years, Bret thought. Most girls her age would have caused a scandal worthy of news media. Addy wasn't like that and it made Bret feel even worse for having taken away her innocence. Say what she will, she could not have known that the comfort he offered her would lead where it did.

The two said no more, only sat by the pond until the wind picked up then slowly headed back across the footpath to the main house to begin the process of forgetting.

Chapter 24

The reunion with Drew was what she expected it to be. It was evident that he had missed her terribly. Having missed him equally as much, she was glad to be with him again. She only wished the day had not been overshadowed with the betrayal she hid from him.

They talked of things he had done while out of town and he wanted to know how her birthday had gone. She told him about all the fun things she did however she omitted the fact that she had done them with only Bret. There was no mention of her mother's abandonment or the scene that happened when she arrived home later that night.

Drew didn't seem to catch on to the vacant eyes staring at him. He couldn't know what thoughts ran through her mind as she wondered how long it would be before she felt comfortable carrying this burden around with her. He seemed oblivious to anything other than her presence. He was such a good guy. He would make some lucky girl a great husband someday. Addy knew he would be the kind of husband that she no longer deserved. She would come to him soiled.

Would he know? Would he be able to tell that he wasn't the first person she had made love to? The thought terrified her to her core. She would be no better than her mother if she married a man under false pretenses only for him to learn she was something completely different than what she let on. She wasn't sure she could do that to Drew. She was equally as sure that she couldn't tell him the truth because her future was not the only one that would be affected if her secret came out. No, she had to keep quiet. She would learn to live with it and she would spend every day trying to make it up to him in other ways. He could never know her reasoning behind certain things but at least it would ease her conscience.

It seemed that Bret had made the same decision and attempted to rectify his relationship with Joanie as well because, when Addy returned home late that night from Drew's place, her mother met her in the upstairs hallway with a look of elation on her face. Having not spoken to her since the day she chose to slap her daughter, Addy was reluctant to engage her mom. However, it didn't seem to matter what had already happened because Joanie was in a fantastic mood and willing to let bygones be bygones.

"I've been waiting until you got home Addy. Where have you been? I have such exciting news," she gushed grabbing both of her daughter's hands.

"I was at Drew's. He just got home from seeing his Grandmother...."

"Who's Drew?" Joanie interrupted in an irritated voice.

"Drew, my boyfriend. The one I've been hanging out with for months and months now. Don't you remember?"

Joanie waved her hand as if to dismiss any talk of this forgettable Drew person.

"Guess where Bret is taking me? Just guess! I bet you can't guess."

Joanie sounded like a young girl she was so giddy.

"I'm sure I have no idea Mom. Where?"

"Europe! He's finished up all his deadline accounts for now and put the others on hold just so he can take me to Europe. I'm so excited! You know we never really got to have a honeymoon because of the whole situation. He promised a cruise once we got settled but he never found time. Now he's making up for it. We're leaving first thing in the morning and we will be gone for three weeks. Isn't that wonderful? I get to experience Paris during the holidays!"

Her joy was almost infectious until Addy heard the last sentence. She had come close to forgetting that Christmas was around the corner.

"You're not going to be home for Christmas? What am I supposed to do for Christmas if you guys are gone?"

The light in Joanie's eyes turned dark.

"You aren't trying to ruin this for me are you? I really think that when we get back, I need to take you to a therapist so you can get this selfish me-me-me attitude out of your system. I don't know what you're complaining about. Most girls your age would kill to have this big house all to themselves for three weeks. You have Margie to cook for you and Miranda will be in three times a week like normal to make sure the house is taken care of. Bret has also arranged to give you an early Christmas present to make sure you can go where you need to go. It's terribly uncivilized for you to be walking the roads and streets at your age. You aren't a child anymore."

With that being said, her mother reached into her pocket and withdrew a set of keys. They were attached to a key ring that was a large letter 'A'.

"What is this?" she asked her mom. Now she was the one who was irritated.

"They are car keys, silly. Keys to your new car that's sitting in the back garage as we speak."

Addy couldn't believe her ears. Her own car? She had driver's license. Her dad had taken her right after their last birthday together and made sure of that but there was hardly any opportunity to use it. Her mother had worked and went to school in her personal vehicle and her father was mostly out of town. Barring buying an additional car, there wasn't one to use. Her father had promised her a car of her own by the time she turned seventeen but sadly he had not made it long enough to keep that promise. Addy had been content to walk where she needed to go. The places she needed to go these days were limited anyway. She was not a social partaker of things like most people her own age.

"Well, what do you have to say now?" her mother asked triumphantly, as if the new expensive gift made all the difference. Surely a new Mazda was worth a lonely Christmas holiday, right? Before Addy could express her thoughts, her mom stuck her hand back into her pocket and drew out a plastic card.

"I almost forgot to give you this. It's your own personal credit card. Use it for gas in your car or food or clothes or just whatever you choose. It's all yours. I explained to Bret how important it was for you to have your own finances now that you have a car."

Joanie leaned in close as if she were sharing her biggest secret and whispered, "It has no limit so no worries on what you buy."

No limit? No worries? Was this how her mother behaved with Bret's money as well? Did the woman think she married into the Kennedy family?

"Thank you Mom, really, but this is just too much. I can't accept it."

Addy tried to hand the card back to her mom but Joanie just shoved her hand back into her chest, lowered her voice and with a threatening tone hissed, "You WILL take it and you will be grateful. I have had enough of your impetuous whining. Shut it up and go thank Bret on your way out to look at your new car."

Joanie abruptly pivoted and headed down the hall to her own bedroom. Addy could hear her talking to herself out loud about needing to pack and which outfits would be acceptable to take or should she simply have Bret buy her new clothes as they went.

Addy was aware that Bret's family was very well off but she hadn't imagined they could afford all this. She hoped those investments held out because if not, her mother would surely bankrupt the Thomas family fortune before long.

Chapter 25

Heading down the stairs towards the back garage, she noticed Bret sitting in the entertainment room with his feet propped on the couch watching a movie. She walked partially into the room in time to see the man on the screen pull a gun on his foe. Bret didn't see her standing there. She cleared her throat and he turned his head away from the action taking place on the television. Jumping into a sitting position he grabbed the remote and muted the volume to his movie.

"Addy…hey there. What's up?" he asked lightly.

"Not a lot. I was just ordered to go try these out," she said as she dangled the new keys in front of her and plopped down on the far end of the couch.

He smiled knowingly and asked, "So, do you like it?"

"I haven't made it that far yet. I wanted to stop by and tell you thank you first. I also wanted to tell you that the credit card was not necessary but I was told it is unreturnable."

He nodded and replied, "It is necessary and so was the car. I want you to have your freedom. Don't stay here locked away at the mercy of the people around you. You can still enjoy your life."

He said it in a way that told her he felt like it was too late to enjoy his own life. It was like the car was a lifeline to her; his way to rescue her from the same fate as him. She could not begrudge that. If it eased his mind, she was happy to accept.

"So, I hear you're headed out for a romantic trip to Europe in the morning."

She tried to sound friendly but only succeeded in sounding jealous.

"Yes. It's the honeymoon she never got to have and don't worry, we will be back a few days before Christmas. You won't actually be alone on Christmas Day. I wouldn't knowingly do that to you. I just thought it was best to get some distance between you and me so we can both get ourselves back to normal."

He was explaining himself to her and it sounded like a lie. She knew the truth but she couldn't be upset about it. He was running from her. She was trying to do the same. They were both creating an environment for damage control. It was what had to be done.

"That's fine. I understand completely," she replied. "I'll probably take the opportunity to have Drew over and show him the property. We will put up a tree and do other holiday things together. I won't be lonely at all."

Could he tell she was lying? Could he see that the thought of him leaving for three weeks made her sadder than her own mother leaving? If he could tell, he said nothing. He only smiled and said, "I think that's a great idea. You guys have fun. Enjoy your holiday."

The thank you had been said and so had the goodbye. It wasn't direct but it was the most normal goodbye they could manage at the time. It would have to suffice. She rose from the couch still twirling the keys on her index finger, gave him a salute and turned to go see what her new gift looked like.

She found her pretty little two door red Mazda waiting silently in the back garage for her. It was hard not to be more than a little excited about it regardless of the story behind it. She had always wanted a little red sports car and now she had it. She couldn't wait to go show it to Drew.

"Merry Christmas to me," she said as she used the key to unlock the door, unable to keep herself from smiling.

Addy drove over to Drew's home and after a short visit she departed; promising him she would be the one to pick him up for a change for a ride to church.

The next morning Addy rose around 7:00 a.m. hoping to catch her mother and Bret before they left on their trip. She pulled her robe around her and shuffled on bare feet down the hallway. She knocked on her mother's door first. There was no answer. She knocked harder and called out to her mother but she heard no reply. Trying the door handle, she found it locked. Maybe they were eating breakfast. She would run down and see. When she reached the dining room she found it empty. Miranda and Margie were both off on Sundays so the house was silent.

They had left without saying goodbye to her. She shouldn't be surprised. Nobody ever considered her these days; nobody except Drew.

Chapter 26

The three weeks her mother was gone had flown by much quicker than she thought possible. It turned out to be quite nice and not lonely at all. Margie had made it her goal to initiate Addy into her flock.

All Margie's children were grown but she had a number of grandchildren and they ranged from very young to older than Addy. It all started when she found out that Joanie had essentially abandoned her daughter in order to spend the holidays abroad. Margie considered that the work of a horrible parent. She didn't like to think badly of other folks but that woman was just rotten and she couldn't sit by and let that poor girl have no family at Christmas.

Addy had been going to Margie's for dinner several times a week, at Margie's suggestion, and it was great. Addy was getting to know all the grandkids. They played games and she helped the younger ones with their homework when they were over. It was what a real home should be. It wasn't big or fancy but it was cozy and filled with love. Addy would be willing to trade it all for just a little of what Margie's family had.

Her own extended family of aunts, uncles, cousins, and the like were nice people but since her father died, Joanie had systematically pushed all of them away. None of her family on either side even called anymore. Some decided that Joanie was a worthless gold digger who never loved Joe so they stopped calling. The others, who weren't making their judgments on her mom's new marriage, were treated with such disdain that they pulled away. In the middle of it all, Addy was left with no safe harbor from the storm, at least not from her blood relations.

Addy had taken Drew with her several times on her trips to Margie's and they all welcomed him like family. It was easy to enjoy those few weeks and even forget about what had happened before her mother's departure. She had even taken an alter call at church two Sundays before, where she had asked God to forgive her for everything and come into her heart; to accept Jesus Christ as her Lord and Savior.

The electric surge in her body that day was off the charts. She could feel the forgiving power of the Holy Spirit coursing through her veins and she knew her nightmare was over. She had been forgiven and made clean. She could be the kind of girlfriend and future wife Drew deserved. Her outlook was brighter than ever.

Living in the south it's very rare to get snow on Christmas but it just so happened that the weather forecast was calling for the possibility of winter weather or at the very least, freezing rain. Addy hadn't wanted to tempt fate by being out and about in case the weather got too bad so she decided she would stay home alone for the day. She wanted to do some catching up on her reading. There were two books on Bret's shelves that she couldn't wait to get her hands on.

127

She got out of bed and slid on her house slippers. With nobody around there was no need to get officially dressed. She planned to wash her face, go down to eat a bite or two of breakfast and head into the sitting room to read in front of the fire. The perfect cozy day was upon her. She no sooner got her book in hand and positioned herself for comfort when she heard a car pull up outside.

Who could that be? She rose to see who it was and suddenly a huge wave of nausea brought her to her knees. She wiped her forehead with the back of her hand and dropped her book. She didn't feel very good at all. Her breakfast obviously did not agree with her. She stood up straight and took a deep breath trying to swallow down the urge to vomit.

The foyer suddenly exploded with the sounds of people and bags being dropped on the tile. She could hear her mother and Bret talking. They were home. Was it that time already, she thought?

"Hello is there anyone around this place?" she heard her mom yelling.

"I'm in here Mom," she unenthusiastically replied. Her mother came breezing through the entryway wearing a new, long fur coat. It was hard to tell what animals had sacrificed their lives for this coat to make its way to the southern part of North America; to a state that rarely gets below forty degrees.

She twirled around like she was putting on a fashion show and exclaimed, "What do you think of my chinchilla coat?"

Before Addy could lie to her and say, 'love it', she stopped in her tracks and dropped her hands to her sides.

"Adelicia, please tell me why you're downstairs in your pajamas like some orphan child from a third world nation." Joanie crossed her arms waiting for an acceptable answer. Addy also noticed her mother's hair had been cut and styled shorter than she had ever seen her wear it. She looked like a totally different woman.

"I forgot what day it was and I didn't think t would matter since I was home alone."

Even as she explained her reasoning to her mom she knew it would not be good enough and wondered why she had even tried to speak at all.

"I worry about you Addy. You really should have more self-esteem. Anyway, I'm completely wiped out and I'm going upstairs to unpack and nap."

She turned to leave her daughter without a hug, a kiss, an exclamation of how much she was missed; nothing. Addy stood there dumbfounded yet again and still a bit more sick to her stomach than she considered normal.

She decided to return the book to the shelf so she could go to her room and get properly dressed for whoever decided to show up at their house during a winter storm. It seemed that the mailman must be important enough to warrant evening wear, she thought grumpily.

After making the trek back to her suite of rooms she was feeling a bit better. Discarding her robe and pajamas in the bathroom, she ran a hot shower and stepped in. The water felt wonderful washing down on her. She had really wanted to tell her mom about her experience at church. She wanted her to know that she had made a decision to give her life to God but she would wait for the right time. She also knew her mother wouldn't see her anymore today so she would have to find a chance to tell her later. As soon as she stepped out of the shower, the sickening nausea returned, only this time much worse than before. Dripping wet, she ran to the toilet, fell onto her knees and vomited repeatedly. It seemed it would never stop. Addy looked at her toes to make sure she hadn't wretched up her toenail polish too. What was wrong with her? Dear God, let it pass, she silently prayed.

Once the feeling had passed, she rose from the floor and finished drying herself off. She got dressed and decided to lie down for just a little while.

Addy was awoken by the sound of someone knocking loudly on her outer door. She felt so groggy and tired. It took all of her willpower just to get up and go to the door. It was Margie.

"Hi sweetie. I came to check on you and find out if you're hungry. You didn't come down for lunch and I haven't seen you all evening."

Margie stood in front of her, nervously wringing her hands. She had that mother hen look on her face. The kind of look that won't take no for an answer when she orders you to take your medicine.

"Lunch? It's already lunch time? I can't believe I slept that long," Addy growled smoothing out her shirt. Margie reached out and laid her palm to Addy's forehead, feeling for a fever she assumed.

"What are you doing Margie? Why are you looking at me like I've got the swine flu or something?"

Margie continued to squint and look the girl over as she said, "I'm looking for a fever because lunch was over four hours ago girl. You've been up here asleep all day. You've got to be sick or something."

All day? She had thought she just took a simple nap, nothing more. Now she finds out she's been asleep *all day*. How weird! Combined with her vomiting earlier this morning, she was sure she was coming down with something. Once she told Margie about the nausea she was ordered back into bed and within minutes she had a tray of hot tea and crackers to calm her rebellious tummy. Margie had taken her temperature and found it to be normal. Her orders were to stay in bed, rest and call if she needed anything in between. It felt good to have someone take care of her like her mom used to when she was young. Oh how she missed that life sometimes. It was sad when your cook noticed you missing for a day and your own mother didn't.

Chapter 27

Addy's symptoms continued on and off for the next week. They seemed to just come and go with no real pattern. She varied between great bouts of energy and lows so deep that she often caught herself falling asleep sitting up. The nausea wasn't as bad as long as she ate regularly, which seemed strange in itself.

The first mention of Addy being sick sent Joanie running back into her rooms claiming that any germs could ruin her complexion. She refused to be around anyone who was sick. There were magazines all over her sitting room that told how germs destroy the antioxidants that keep you young. Joanie was obsessed with not only stopping father time but turning back the hands of his clock. Her comments were that she had done her duty and wiped Addy's runny nose one too many times in her childhood, she wouldn't be available to do it again.

No, it was Margie who doctored Addy and Margie who made sure she ate. The woman was a saint. She counted her blessings every day when it came to Margie. God had put that wonderful woman in her life on purpose.

Drew had been by after she missed a few days of school. He was of course concerned for her health but she assured him it would pass. They spent an evening or two playing video games in the entertainment room until she was tired out and begged fatigue. She tried to introduce him to Joanie once while he was visiting but the meeting fell flat when her mother stated she couldn't be bothered to socialize because she was leaving for a silent auction with her friend Jill. She halfheartedly waved at the two of them and mouthed 'Ta Ta everyone' as she sashayed out the door. So much for her mother getting to know the boy she loved.

Bret had dropped in to say hello a few times as well but she noticed that he spent less time working and more time drinking in the entertainment room. She never saw him use the gym equipment anymore and he hardly ever entered his office. There were times when she could tell that he wanted to say something to her but she never gave him the chance. He was behaving like a man in mourning and Addy had put all of that behind her. She would pray for Bret in hopes that he could do the same. Things would turn around for him just like they did for her, she was positive.

Several days into the new year, Addy was up in her suite rummaging through her sitting room looking for an earring she lost when Bret entered her room.

"Hi. Can we talk?"

She didn't know what he wanted and it made her uncomfortable for him to be staring at the sofa in such an intense way. To her, it appeared he was trying to conjure up an instant replay.

"Sure. What's up?" she asked, deliberately sitting down in her recliner so there would be no place for him to sit close to her. Even though he was seated several feet away she could smell the alcohol on his breath. The odor threatened to cause her nausea to return. She tried to swallow down the urge and hoped it would fade away. She wondered, 'How early was he taking his first drink these days?'

"I can't do it Addy. I can't go on this way. I hate her. I really hate her. She whined the whole trip. She shopped continuously and when I tried to do something romantic with her, she shooed me away like a fly. It was like being her bellhop while she was on vacation. I don't know what I thought it would accomplish by taking that trip. I really don't know what I expected but I do know what I got and I can't do it anymore. She's a monster. I see that now. I know now it's you Addy. I need you, not her. Let's leave. We can go away together. We can go somewhere that no one knows our circumstances. I'll call my parents and they will help. I just know it. Please say yes."

He sounded like a man who was pleading for his life at the end of a gun barrel. She didn't know what to do. She thought he had moved on like she had and now he was here baring his soul to her. But this time, it wasn't what she wanted to hear.

"Bret, you're not thinking clearly. You've been drinking. Why don't you go sleep it off and in the morning you will see that you don't really feel this way."

He stood up quickly and venomously spat, "I'm NOT drunk! Don't tell me how I feel!"

Bret had never spoken to her so harshly before. She didn't know how to talk to him this way. She stood up and held out her hands.

"I'm sorry. I wasn't trying to tell you what to do. I promise. I was just trying to get you to give yourself some time to think; maybe a bit more clearly than you are right now."

She was trying to talk him down like someone who was threatening to jump off of a ledge. This was insane to her. She never believed in a million years she would be standing in front of a young and handsome stepfather begging him not to throw his life away for the love of her. It never occurred to her that stretching out her hands in his direction would give him ample opportunity to ensnare her, but it did. With lightning fast reflexes Bret pulled her to him and tried to kiss her. Her mind had not even processed it before she was already in his embrace and smelling the gin on his breath. The gagging sensation was returning as she struggled and squirmed.

"Stop Bret, please! Let me go! STOP!"

Addy pleaded these words over and over and she tried with all her strength to push against his chest and free herself. Yes, Bret had been drinking but even in his drunken state he was still stronger than she was, especially with her recent sickness weakening her. Try as she might, she couldn't get free.

His hands groped her as he mumbled words of love and devotion. He called her name one minute and her mother's name the next. She had already begun to cry when she realized he was no longer hearing her. Her heart was racing so fast she felt dizzy. Her face felt hot. Within seconds she began to feel tingling in her hands and suddenly everything went black.

Chapter 28

The light hurt like little pins sticking in her eyes. She could see it coming through the blind slits as she woke up. Her head was killing her. Where was she? Looking to her right she saw Margie talking to a doctor by the door.

A hospital. She was in a hospital. Why? What exactly had happened? Margie glanced over to see Addy peering around confused. She quickly came to her bedside. The doctor excused himself silently.

"Oh thank God you're awake! I was so worried about you sweetheart," Margie said as relief swept over her and she patted Addy's hand.

"What happened? Why am I here? Where's mom?"

Poor girl, Margie thought. She didn't deserve the hand she had been dealt. She sighed and said, "Honey your momma is still at home. She wouldn't come to the hospital with us; you know how she is with germs and all."

She did know, very well.

"Mr. Thomas came running down telling me he called 911 because he found you passed out in your room.

He was worried to death. When the ambulance got there I asked to ride with you and he sent me on over here. You've been out for almost an hour."

Little by little the memory was creeping back in. She did remember now. Bret had barged in to her room, drunk, and she had obviously had a panic attack. How could he scare her like that?

The doctor she had seen talking with Margie a few minutes earlier had returned to the room with his clipboard. He was a tall skinny man with a long nose. His expression was one of concern but she wasn't sure to what degree. She could tell him what she ailed from, it was called neglect.

"Addy, I'm Dr. Bishop. It's good to see you awake. How do you feel? Any pain or discomfort anywhere?" He pressed under her jaw and behind her ears as he asked his questions.

"My head hurts, I guess. Did I have an anxiety attack or something?" she asked. He nodded as if he fully expected her head to hurt and was not surprised. He briefly scribbled on his pad.

"Addy I need to speak with you alone about some tests we performed."

The doctor was implying that Margie would have to go and Addy was not letting that happen. This woman was the closest thing she had to a mother and she wanted her to be here for whatever he planned on telling her. Margie grabbed her purse and threw it over her shoulder to exit the room.

"Wait! I want her to be here for anything you tell me please."

Margie looked from the doctor to Addy, waiting to see if he would allow it or not. After a few seconds the doctor nodded and said, "So be it. Miss McMullen you came in unconscious, having a recent history of fatigue, loss of appetite, vomiting and several other symptoms so we felt it necessary to run a blood panel to determine what we might be dealing with."

The doctor paused dramatically. Addy couldn't understand all the hype over a panic attack. She had bigger issues on her plate right now than anxiety.

"What I'm trying to tell you Addy is that the results of your blood work confirm that you are pregnant. Without a proper vaginal exam I would guess, due to your hormone levels, you should be about five weeks along."

If there was a sound you could make that defined disbelief, she would have made it. Margie continued to hold her hand as she stared blankly at this man who was obviously joking with her.

"That isn't possible," she muttered.

"Are you saying that you have *never* engaged in sexual activity Miss McMullen?" the doctor asked suspiciously.

"Yes. I mean, no. I mean...once...but I can't be pregnant," she wailed.

"Oh but I'm afraid it *is* possible dear and you *are* most positively pregnant. That explains all your symptoms as well as your fainting spell. Other than a baby on board, your blood work suggests you are healthy as a horse. We will refer you to a local OB-GYN for an intake appointment."

He scribbled a few more notes on his clipboard and smiled, saying, "Congratulations. I hope you feel better soon," as he left the room.

Silence. Neither she nor Margie wanted to be the first to speak. She thought, 'Congratulations? On what?' On the worst disaster in her entire life? Congratulations on singlehandedly ruining the lives of everyone she loved? Finally someone had to break the ice and it was Margie.

"Addy honey, it's going to be okay. Drew is a wonderful boy and I know it's unexpected but he will do right by the both of you. I just know it."

She thinks it's Drew's baby, Addy thought. How could she tell her the truth? How would she tell everyone the truth? How was this happening to her? She had done what was right. She had asked God for forgiveness. She had been loyal and good. Why had God punished her this way? She could only cry. Margie tried to comfort her with words of encouragement but deep inside she knew what a wretched human being she was and when that sweet woman found her out, she would think so too.

Once she was discharged, Margie had called a cab to take them home. It was a ride she would never forget. The entire way home she thought of nothing else but how she would tell all these people about the hard cold proof of her sins. Could she go through with it? She had to; there was no other option at this point.

Chapter 29

After the taxi pulled away, Addy stopped on the front portico and turned to Margie.

"Please don't say anything. I'll tell them. I promise. I just want to do it my way."

Margie nodded and agreed that it was never her place to relay such a secret anyway. She did tell Addy that no matter what, she would always be there for her if she needed anything at all.

"You're like one of my own granddaughters," she told her.

Addy thanked her for everything and excused herself to her room but this time she locked the doors. She did not want to see anyone or talk to anyone else until she could decide what to do. It all made sense to her now. She hadn't even noticed that she missed her period a couple weeks ago. She thought the sickness was just something she ate. She never had the slightest inkling that she could be growing another human being inside of her. She felt stupid for not thinking of it. She wasn't an idiot. She knew where babies came from but for some reason she never worried that she would suffer those consequences from her one night with Bret. She could see how wrong she was. She would reap the harvest of sin that she sowed.

She found herself staring into her full length mirror, trying to imagine what she would look like when the time came that she could no longer hide her secret. As a young girl she had dreamed of the day when she would pop the news to her husband that they were going to have a baby. The thoughts had always been so exciting and tender. They were nothing at all like the reality that was now hers. Addy knew that whichever road she decided to take, she needed to know all of her options; just in case. The only way to get started on that was to wait until she went to her intake appointment. She could talk with the doctor and have all the information she needed to face her mother and Bret.

Three days later, Addy excused herself early from school to be able to make her very first appointment with the obstetrician. Her doctor, thankfully, was a woman. She wasn't sure she could feel comfortable with a man considering her delicate situation.

The exam was extremely uncomfortable and just as humiliating. Dr. Taylor assured her that all women have the same exams when they're pregnant and it's totally normal. She didn't think the doctor was lying but she sure couldn't see it ever becoming no big deal. Having another person rooting around up there made her feel like they were hillbilly hand fishing. She was not a fan of fishing in any form.

All the tests and measurements seemed to coincide with the prediction she received at the emergency room several days earlier. Addy was right on the cusp of being six weeks pregnant. Her due date would be late August.

"Dr. Taylor, can I ask you something?" she whispered. The doctor finished pulling off her exam gloves and sat down by Addy.

"Sure you can. Fire away." She was a nice lady and Addy felt like she could trust her completely; not just because she was a doctor but because she seemed like a sincerely good lady.

"If I didn't want to keep it, who would I talk to?"

This question didn't shock Dr. Taylor. She dealt with this type of thing very often. She couldn't count the number of young girls who came through her office each year that with accidental pregnancies but without the resources or the desire to be a parent.

"That depends on what you mean when you say you don't want to keep it. Do you mean adoption or abortion?"

Just hearing the words come out of her mouth made Addy feel sick inside. What kind of person does this? She knew what she was doing and now that there was a baby in the picture, she was considering bailing out. She was ashamed of herself.

"Can you give me information on all of it please?"

The nice doctor swiveled around in her chair and opened a cabinet drawer. She fished out several pamphlets and a few sheets of paperwork.

"These cover all the options available to people in your situation. If you have any questions please call our office. If I'm not available, one of my nurses will be glad to answer anything for you.

Addy sat in her car for over an hour before leaving the parking lot. She read all of the literature, crying as she went along. Why did it have to be so hard to decide? She knew she had to tell Bret. She wanted to pretend this was not happening but that was not realistic. She wiped her eyes and nose before starting her car. She was heading home to do what she knew had to be done.

"Dear God, if you don't hate me too bad for what I've done, please help me figure this out," she whispered to the empty interior around her.

Chapter 30

Bret was not in his office when she arrived and surprisingly he wasn't in the entertainment room either. She knew he was definitely somewhere on the property because his car was parked outside. He hadn't even pulled it into the front garage, but had left it in the drive instead.

Once a search of the whole house yielded nothing, she went to the last room that remained unchecked, the workout room. She found Bret inside, sitting on the ab machine with his feet propped up. He was drinking a beer. He held up his beverage in her direction when she entered, as if toasting her arrival.

"I've found a new way to get pumped up. Whatchya think?" he joked. When she didn't laugh he swung his legs off the equipment and turned her way.

"I need to talk to you. It's important," she said.

"If you're going to tell me I'm a horrible person for avoiding you since the other day, I know. I didn't mean to hurt you. I was drinking and I got carried away," he recited his statement as if he had been prepared for this apology for days. He knew she would seek him out when she felt comfortable to be around him again.

He had made a colossal mess out of everything and he couldn't seem to stop himself. He even considered offering to move her to a boarding school just to keep her safe from his own impulsive actions.

She sat across from him on a small bench where she could face him during this conversation.

"That isn't what I want to talk with you about. What I have to say is much more important and very serious so I need you to hear me out."

The dire tone in her voice could not be denied. Whatever she had come to say was going to impact him severely, he could feel it.

"When I passed out the other day, you didn't cause it. I guess technically you did but it wasn't anything you did that day. I passed out because I'm pregnant. I had a follow-up appointment today with an obstetrician and she confirmed it. I'm six weeks along. You are the father Bret; you're the only person I've ever been with."

Addy paused to give Bret a chance to let this information sink in. She didn't expect it to be easy for him. It had been terribly hard for her own mind to grasp it. After several seconds she continued to talk.

"I have information on our options. We can do regular adoption or blind adoption. We can also get in touch with organizations that can place the baby even before it's born. We could work hand-in-hand with the adoptive parents. I won't have it until late summer so it shouldn't affect my schooling. I can tell my mother that I don't know who it belongs to. She hates me anyway. She probably already thinks I'm sleeping with half the county. I've given it a lot of thought and I'm willing to take the bullet on this."

Bret sat his beer down on the floor beside his feet.

"Take the bullet? No way. This is my baby and I want it. You can't legally give my child away Addy. This isn't your teen drama production. Your mom has already taken enough of my future away. I'll be damned if I let you do it too."

She could see his anger mounting.

"I'm not trying to make you mad but you know as well as I do that we would never be able to keep this baby. It wouldn't work. It would ruin your life and the baby's life too. Please don't do this Bret. Please, you have to listen to reason," she pleaded.

Suddenly the hair on her arms stood up. They were not alone. She turned to see exactly where Bret's gaze was focused. In the doorway, her mother silently stood listening to their entire conversation. Once Joanie knew she was revealed, she continued into the room. The look on her face was one of pure wrath. Addy began to tremble but didn't dare move a muscle.

"Well well, someone forgot to invite me to the family fun day it seems."

Joanie slowly walked in circles around the two of them like a lioness stalking her prey. The smile on her face was macabre and out of place. Her plum lip color made her resemble a deranged clown.

"I'm always the last to know the juicy gossip around here but, I must say, this one takes the prize. I feel so tacky coming here without a congratulations gift for my new grandchild; or is it my new stepchild? I can't seem to determine which way that would go."

Her tone was light, like they were all playing a game of charades and any minute someone would guess correctly and the round would be over. This unsettled Addy tremendously.

"You know, Miranda tried to tell me what was going on in my own home, under my nose. But she's such a suck up I just considered it an overplayed attempt to win my confidence. I never believed her. Guess the maid had it right the whole time. I never heard a peep out of dear old Margie about it. She of course worships the ground

146

that your slutty little feet walk on," she directed the last comment at her daughter.

Bret had been bullied long enough by this woman and he decided he would not let it go on any longer.

"You watch your mouth Joanie. You don't know anything about this and you have no right to come in here acting like you're anyone's mother or anyone's wife. You quit being both of those things a long time ago."

Her eyebrows raised, surprised that he had the stones to stand up to her at what would be his weakest moment yet.

"You don't think I have any right huh? Well dear, let me tell you what *my* rights are. I have the right to divorce you for adultery, have you arrested for statutory rape, interference with child custody, and wipe out your family reputation in the media. Don't forget that when I do all of this, the courts will feel so sorry for poor little me that I will walk away with most of your money, your real estate holdings and this house too. If you think I'm bluffing, I suggest you try me."

She actually looked like she was pleased with herself for knowing exactly how to destroy her husband. She also had more to say because she pointed her finger at her daughter and said, "You *will* destroy that *thing* you're carrying and you'll do it quietly. Once the deed is done you will go to a private school where you can finish your education away from here. Understand that the only reason I'm offering you this is to keep the public from knowing what trash my only child has become. If you choose not to do this, I will tell everyone how you seduced my husband to get pregnant and take him from me. No one will speak to you again. You'll have no family, no home and no income. It's very hard for a pregnant homeless teenager to find work. From this moment on, you are dead to me…just like Joe."

Joanie plunged her index finger into Addy's chest to make her point. The adrenaline was coursing through

Addy's veins and she was feeling faint and flush with anger. Her mother was officially the most hideous person she had ever known. She had not deserved her dad, Addy thought. She didn't deserve her daughter. She certainly didn't deserve this precious little baby she would bring into this world. In a split second Addy had acted before she thought.

Taking both hands she shoved outward towards her mother and connected with her breast bone, propelling Joanie backwards. When she realized her daughter had pushed her she attempted to catch her balance but instead it only made her fall with more force. A set of free weights caught her fall but it appeared to have also caught the side of Joanie's head. She was unconscious and bleeding steadily from her right temple. Her right arm was contorted in an unnatural way underneath her body.

What had she done? She hadn't meant to push her at all, much less as hard as she did. Bret was over top of his wife calling her name, trying to wake her up. Addy could hear him shouting to her, "Call 9-1-1!"

He shouted again and again but she was paralyzed. Her body was frozen in fear. Finally he took out his cell phone and called them himself. She could hear his side of the call.

"My wife, she's fallen and hit her head and she's bleeding! Please hurry!"

Bret ran over and roughly grabbed Addy by the shoulders, causing her to wince in pain.

"This was an accident. She tripped. You never touched her. Do you hear me?"

He was yelling into her face, of course she heard him. She nodded her agreement and shook his hands away from her shoulders. She sat back down on the bench and continued to stare at her mother, helplessly sprawled on the floor. Addy wondered if her mother was dead. She looked dead; just like the bodies she had seen in movies. Funny, she felt strangely relieved to think her mother

148

might actually be gone. What a horrible thought, to wish one's parent dead. Did good girls do that? No, she didn't think they did.

In moments, Margie was running into the room with Bret on her heels. She gathered Addy with the intent of shuffling her upstairs away from the arriving ambulance. Margie had no idea that anyone else knew Addy's condition so she wanted to ensure no harm came to the baby by such an upsetting accident.

Margie had gotten Addy to lie down on her bed and pulled a blanket over her. It wasn't long before the entire driveway was filled with the flashing red and blue lights of first responders. She could hear the sound of doors slamming and radio static from downstairs. Addy laid somber and quiet in her bed, staring out her large windows. She could see them loading her mother into the ambulance. She was strapped to a gurney but there was no body bag around her. That was a good sign that she was alive.

Margie could only feel concern for this girl. She could tell that there was no sign of panic in Addy. Having the kind of heartless woman she had for a mother, she didn't wonder at all why the child wasn't upset. She was ashamed to admit that it would probably be better for everyone if the accident had a more final result. Margie was not the kind of woman to wish such things on people but pretending the truth was not the truth had never helped anyone.

Bret had come upstairs to tell Margie that he was following the ambulance to the emergency room. She was under strict orders not to allow Addy out of bed. He wanted her resting and not worrying. He promised to phone as soon as he knew anything.

149

Chapter 31

Despite protests from Addy, Margie decided to stay the night with her. Bret had called to say that her mother had sustained a serious blow to the head and remained unconscious. The doctors had been running tests all evening and were telling him that until some of the swelling in her brain reduced, they would not know her prognosis.

Margie had made her some dinner but she didn't have an appetite. A few bites of pot roast were all she could stomach. Drew called but Margie told him Addy was sleeping. She filled him in on the accident and promised to have Addy return his call when she awoke the next morning.

"I'm just not comfortable with waking her up Drew. She's had such an awful day and she needs rest in her condition."

She had not meant to say that.

"Her condition? What do you mean Margie?" he asked worriedly.

Thank goodness they were on the phone and not face to face because Margie was a terrible liar and she knew Drew would have been able to see right through her next comment.

"Her nerves are shot and she's been sick this past week. You know that son. She needs rest but I'll tell her you called," she said in a rushed voice, wanting him to hurry up and say his goodbyes before she said anything else she shouldn't say.

"Oh sure. I'm sorry. I understand completely. Tell her we all love her and will be praying for her mom. Please call us if we can help in any way."

Margie thanked the boy. He and his family really were good people. Too bad this bunch around here wasn't like that, she thought. It comforted her to know that Addy would have such a loving family to help her out with the baby. A lot of teen mothers didn't get that lucky.

Bret stayed at the hospital all night. Addy woke up early to find Margie still there.

"What is your family going to think about you staying out all night?" she asked.

"Oh who cares what they say? They know what happened and you're like family to us. They would find it unusual if I *didn't* stay with you. Now take yourself a seat there and let me fix you some nice warm oatmeal. It's good for you and good for the baby too."

Addy cringed at her mention of the baby. She sighed and asked, "Have you heard anything from the hospital or Bret this morning?"

Margie was reaching in the cupboard for the can of oats and replied, "Yes dear. Bret called about a half hour ago and said your mom's still unconscious. The doctors say she's got to wake up in her own time; nobody can force it."

"I'm going to the hospital after I eat. You should go home and see about your family Margie. You can't stop me so you might as well agree with me."

Shooting Addy a disgruntled look she smacked the countertop with a spoon.

"Young lady, you're a pain in my butt," she jokingly replied.

Addy smiled softly letting her know she took no offense at the comment. As Margie poured the oatmeal into a bowl, she remembered Drew's phone call.

"Oh you need to call Drew. He's worried sick. I told him you were sleeping but you would call him this morning."

She didn't reply. Still unable to face Drew, she had simply been avoiding him the past week. Her solution to everything had meant that she would have to cut ties with Drew, letting him believe she had been unfaithful to him and now carried another person's baby. She knew it would have to be that way but she kept putting it off. Today would be no different. She couldn't deal with every crisis at once. Drew would just have to take a back burner yet again.

Finishing her breakfast she went upstairs to change. She had to go to the hospital and face her first priority, her mother.

Addy arrived at the hospital to find Bret sitting in the waiting area sipping on a luke warm cup of stale coffee. His clothing was rumpled and he hadn't slept. The bags under his eyes told the tale of exhaustion. She took a seat beside him. Hospital furniture was most uncomfortable. Did they think if they put anything nice in the waiting rooms that people would never want to leave?

Addy had been forced to wear cotton exercise pants because her jeans were becoming too tight to button comfortably. She didn't look like a pregnant woman but simply someone who was out for a morning jog.

"Any changes?" she asked in a low voice.

"No. The swelling in her brain isn't going down. It's causing other things to go haywire. They aren't telling me much. I told the doctors that she tripped and fell backwards."

"Go home for a while. I'll stay here with her. You need a shower and some fresh clothes. A nap wouldn't hurt either."

She was concerned for him and hoped he would accept her offer, if only for a short while. He needed to rest and it was a fact that neither of them could do anything but wait. They may as well take turns sitting around waiting, she thought.

"You will call me if there's any change? You promise?"

"I swear. Now go." She waved him away and he stood up to stretch.

He was stiff and achy from being in that chair all night. His limbs were screaming for relaxation.

"Thank you Addy. I'm going to take a shower and catch a nap. I won't be long," he promised.

"Take your time," she offered.

After Bret left, one of the nurses came to the waiting room looking for him. She called his name out and Addy jumped up.

"He's not here but that's my mother in there. I'm Addy. Is there something wrong?" she quickly asked.

The nurse gently touched Addy's arm and said, "No dear. I was just coming out to let him know that your mom's stable enough for a short visit if he or you are up to it."

"Oh yes," she replied. "Is she finally awake?"

The nurse sadly shook her head to signify that she would not be awake for the visit.

"I'm sorry but your mom is still in a coma. She has significant swelling in the brain caused by her fall. She's only just now become stable enough for us to allow visitors. Keep in mind though, she is still very critical and not out of the woods yet."

"Yes ma'am," Addy replied while following the nice nurse through a set of double doors that required a code to open them. The nurse motioned towards the second little glass room on the left.

Inside the little cubicle, her mother was lying in bed, hooked up to a number of machines. Her eyes were closed and her face looked unusually puffy. Her pallor was a greenish gray color and her lips were tinted blue. The hospital staff had wiped away all of her makeup and a bandage had been expertly wrapped around her head. The woman lying on this intensive care bed looked like the mother that Addy had long ago forgotten. The sight of her in this condition pulled so many memories to the surface. The mother who brushed out her pig tails before school couldn't be the same mother who attacked her with cruel and vengeful words less than twenty-four hours ago. Addy stood at her bedside and gently touched the only spot on her mother's hand that was not taped up with tubes leading to IV bags.

"Mom, I'm so sorry. I know everything went wrong with us but I'm so sorry. Please wake up. If you still hate me when you wake up I'll understand but I can't lose you. You're still my mom and I need you. Bret needs you. Please...." she whispered in Joanie's ear.

No response. The only sounds in the air were the constant 'shhhip...shhhip...shhhip' sound of the respirator helping her mother breathe. The occasional low beeping tone could be heard from one of her IV dispensers. Part of her expected her mom to wake up at the sound of her voice. The other part remembered that her mom probably didn't *want* to wake up for her and it made her sad.

It seemed like only seconds before the nurse returned and told her that visiting time was over. She leaned forward and kissed her mother on the forehead, whispering to her that she would be back soon.

154

Chapter 32

Addy grew weary as she waited for more news but none came. The magazines at her disposal were several years old and she had read them all…twice. Her mother's condition had apparently not changed since her short visit because no one had come out to give her any updates. Surely someone would alert her, wouldn't they?

Drew called her cell phone several times that day but each call was sent to voicemail. He repeatedly left messages and texted, desperate for a reply. She knew she should take his calls but she was being a coward; putting off the inevitable. She would add that to her list of things to be ashamed of but right now she just couldn't take one more straw on her back. She was becoming overwhelmed with it all.

Bret called about twenty minutes earlier letting Addy know that he was on his way back to the hospital. He insisted on apologizing at least three times for not returning sooner.

"Stop saying you're sorry," she scolded. "Your four hour nap was very little of what you actually needed. I told you to take as long as you want. I wasn't going anywhere."

"I know but this is my responsibility, not yours. I want you as far away from this as possible, especially when your mom wakes up. You know anything could happen."

He was still trying to protect her. She really appreciated it but she also knew that when her mom woke up, it could go either way. Addy couldn't and wouldn't blame Joanie for turning in her daughter. She knew she had acted on her anger. She also knew that she was in the wrong; willing to be blamed and punished.

Bret appeared a short time after his telephone call. He was looking fresh and much more relaxed. Like Addy, he had chosen to wear a nice track suit. She liked how casually suave he looked.

"So have they updated you yet?" Bret immediately asked her.

"No change. I got to see her for just a few minutes right after you left but don't panic, she wouldn't wake up," she confided.

"Why didn't you call me? What would you have done if she woke up with you there alone? What if she started screaming about what you did?"

His questions were annoying to her but they made a real point. She didn't know what she would do if any of those things happened. Bret was right. She had to be careful not to stir up any memory her mom may have of her accident.

The waiting room was unusually empty. With the exception of an older couple napping at the other side of the room, Addy and Bret were alone together. She stood and went over to the coffee maker to brew another pot of communal coffee. Filling the pot with water she looked across the room and was surprised to see Drew stepping into the waiting room, obviously looking for her. She raised her hand up to get his attention and he beamed his smile as brightly as ever. That smile broke her heart.

Drew came straight ahead and extended his arms for her to lean into them. She had avoided him for too long and now he had decided to come to her. It was stupid of her to think he wouldn't eventually show up at the hospital. It was not his style to be away from his girlfriend during a crisis. The two embraced as he told her how sorry he was that he had not been there sooner.

"It's okay Drew. I'm fine, just a bit tired," she told him.

"My poor girl. Have you heard anything new today? Is she making any progress?"

Addy gently pulled away from his embrace and replied, "No. They haven't told us anything so far. It's been a long day."

Drew noticed her aloof behavior but he simply assumed she was worried about her mother. He couldn't possibly imagine what reasons were behind those eyes. Bret arose and walked over to shake Drew's hand.

"Thanks for coming Drew. We really appreciate it," he said as he pumped Drew's hand up and down.

The three of them stood by making small talk for a few moments until someone called out from the doorway, "Family of Joanie Thomas. Is there anyone in here that is the family of Joanie Thomas?"

Addy grabbed her purse and shouted, "That's us, over here!"

The nurse motioned for them to follow her out into the hallway. Joanie must finally be awake, Bret thought.

Chapter 33

The group of three gathered in a semi- circle around the nurse to hear what she had to say.

"Who is the husband?" she asked looking back and forth from Bret to Drew. Obviously someone had told her that 'the husband' was much younger because she didn't seem surprised that it might be either of them. Bret raised his hand. She directed her conversation to him since he was Joanie's legal representative.

"Your wife is not doing well Mr. Thomas. The pressure on her brain has not reduced. The swelling has caused complications in other areas. The brain is the hub for all working things in the body and when the hub isn't functioning correctly, nothing else will either. Her blood pressure has spiked to dangerous levels regardless of the medication we are giving her. It's also affecting her internal organs. Tests show decreased kidney and liver functions. We can go in, drill a hole in her skull to try and relieve some pressure but we don't believe it will affect the organs fast enough to stop damage or a possible shut down. We also cannot be sure that she will ever even wake up at this point."

The nurse paused and looked from Bret to Addy and from Addy to Drew. She was waiting for confirmation that they had understood what she was telling them.

"So are you saying that my mother may be brain dead? Are you saying that she's dying?" Addy asked in a shaky voice.

"What I'm saying is that right now your mother is what we consider brain dead. Could she wake up? Well, miracles do happen but medically we see no viable chance. Is she dying per se? She could die from organ failure or we could contain the organ failure and stop any further damage but would she wake up? Most likely not. She would only be alive hooked up to machines that make her heart beat. Her brain can no longer tell her heart to beat or her lungs to breathe."

A small cry escaped Addy's lips. She felt as if she were falling down a long tunnel with no end. This was all her fault. She had pushed he; she had murdered her own mother. She didn't deserve to live.

Addy stumbled backwards trying to get as far away as she could. Her ears were ringing and she felt like she would vomit any second. She reached out to steady herself on anything close by but before she could balance, everything went black. She had passed out.

Addy woke up on a gurney in the hallway with a nurse taking her pulse. Bret and Drew were standing behind the nurse waiting.

"There you are," the nurse said when she opened her eyes. Addy tried to sit up but the nurse held her hand on her arm to keep her down.

"Not yet. You took a hard spill. You just lie still for a minute or two. Your stepfather told us you had been seen here before so we pulled your chart just in case it wasn't a simple fainting spell. Thankfully that's all we

159

think it is. Your pulse and your blood pressure are all within normal range. I do always advise all of my pregnant patients to get checked out by your own OB anytime you take a fall like that."

Drew's eyes shot wide open and his jaw dropped. She could see him out of the corner of her eye. His breathing was becoming rapid and she knew he was extremely confused by what he just heard. The nurse helped her into a sitting position and told her to get some rest before she made her exit.

"Addy, what did she just say to you? Why did she say you were pregnant? Why didn't you correct her?"

Drew was becoming impatient for her to answer his arsenal of questions.

"Addy, I don't understand. Why are you not answering me?"

Her guilt ravaged expression told him all he needed to know. She opened her mouth to offer something, anything close to an explanation, but before any words could come out Drew closed his eyes and held both hands in front of his face as if trying to shield himself from what was coming next.

"Don't! Just don't say it," he yelled.

The other nurses standing at a nearby desk turned to see what the yelling was about but none of them tried to intervene. Bret moved behind Addy to steady her just in case she decided to have a spontaneous fainting spell again. The tears that had worked their way to the surface were spilling down both of her cheeks. Her chest felt like someone had dropped an anvil on top of it. The pain was almost unbearable.

"Drew, please," she cried softly.

"No," he spat with venom. "I trusted you. I believed in you. I made a promise to you and you made a promise to me. How could you go to church with me in front of God and my family and be having sex with someone behind my back?"

160

Watching Drew's pain was enough to break the strongest person. He had loved this girl with every ounce of his energy and she had betrayed him. He didn't even want to know who she chose to do it with. It didn't matter. It didn't change the facts. She opened her mouth again and reached out to Drew. With blinding speed, he jerked away from her and pointed his finger into her face.

"Don't touch me. Don't ever touch me again. I never want to see you or speak to you again! I don't associate with whores. Lose my number and my address," he added as he turned and strode quickly away.

In less than thirty minutes time, she had been told that her actions had caused the death of her only living parent and she lost the only truly good thing she had in her life, her boyfriend. Her legs started to shake as sobs wracked her body and Bret swiftly caught her weight. He maneuvered her into a chair in the waiting room where he leaned into her gaze.

"This is not your fault Addy. Do you hear me?"

She was crying harder by the second. He didn't think she heard anything. If she did, she wasn't responding to him.

"Addy, please stop crying. We will get through this together. We have each other and we have our baby."

His words were like cold water poured over her head. Our baby? My God, what had she done? The impact of everything came crashing down on her at once. She jumped to her feet and ran. She could hear Bret calling after her as she fled the waiting room but if he gave chase she didn't notice. She ran out into the street and continued to flee into the night. The farther she ran the harder she cried. She voices inside her head each telling her so many things; it was chaos.

'This is all your fault,' said one voice.

'You don't deserve to live,' said another.

'The world and this baby would be better off if you were dead,' reminded yet another voice.

161

Once upon a time Addy had been an avid jogger but not so much lately. She ran until she becoming extremely winded and her side began to hurt. As she started slowing down to catch her breath, she realized that she had run in the direction of the county line. She felt foolish.

It was freezing outside and she had only a light fleece jacket keeping her from the cold. Her car was still parked in the hospital parking lot and her purse was in the waiting room. When she ran out, she left it all. Somewhere in her subconscious she knew she wouldn't need any of it anymore. She had already made up her mind; she just hadn't known it until that very moment. It was suddenly clear what her only option was.

She continued to follow the road that would lead her to the county line. It was becoming colder with each she took into the dark night. She couldn't recall how low the temperatures were supposed to get but she knew they were going to be frigid. Her face burned from the cold wind as she walked on the side of the narrow two-lane county road. Once she reached her destination she knew she would be staring head on towards the Flaggers Bridge.

The bridge was the physical divider between Polton and Despin counties. All her life she had heard the grown-ups joke about how far down the bridge you had to actually be before you were considered out of the county. It was a great old bridge left over from a time when it was a new practice to make bridges out of steel. She remembered her father telling her once that he remembered her Grandfather spinning stories of the days when that bridge had only wooden rails on the sides. The thought was scary because it was a large bridge and she always thought it would be easy for someone to drive off the side, were it not for the steel rails that now adorned it.

It was fitting to Addy that this beautiful bridge of her childhood would be the last place she ever saw on this earth. She could not go on living with the knowledge of what she had done. She couldn't bring a child into such a dysfunctional situation. She would never forgive herself. She had let down her father's memory. She had let down her family but most of all, she had let down God and she didn't deserve his forgiveness. She had been too bad of a person.

Her mind was made up.

Tonight was the night when she would climb up the side of the Flaggers Bridge and jump over into the icy waters below. She had found herself researching such a method of suicide in the past week, learning all she could. She tried to tell herself that she was simply curious but deep down she had already known what her plans were. She just didn't know *when* it would happen.

Now she knew.

Addy reached the bridge very late that night. She stood staring out over the water thinking back on the life she had lived, sad that it had been so short yet so tragic.

Chapter 34

The events that led to her being up on the side of that bridge were things she didn't want to talk about with this nice couple who had saved her life last night. She couldn't tell them what had happened. How do you inform someone you've just met that you're pregnant with your stepfather's baby and you killed your mother? It makes for uncomfortable dinner conversation.

She had to decide something because she couldn't go back. She wouldn't go back. They couldn't make her. Then again, what choice did she have? She had to get up, go downstairs, and face the people who had felt that her life was worth living. What she would tell them wasn't important right now. The only thing that mattered was that she took the first step toward making sense out of this whole thing.

Pulling herself out of bed she could feel her sore stiff joints screaming in pain with each flex of her muscles. Running six miles and climbing a bridge in hypothermic conditions could leave a person feeling a little less than great the next morning. The clothes Helen had given her to sleep in were loose, warm and cozy. The fabric was soft from many years of wash and wear.

Someone had to be in the kitchen because the smell of food being cooked had wafted up the stairs and met Addy as soon as she left the little bedroom. She softly padded down the stairs looking for source of the delicious aroma.

The Campbell's had a modest home. She liked it a lot. It reminded her of Margie's house. Addy noticed that there were no pictures of their children on the walls. How odd. Surely people their age had children of their own and even a few grandchildren. Her nose led her to the room she was looking for. When she entered the kitchen, Helen greeted her with a huge smile.

"Good morning dear! Did you sleep well?"

"Oh yes ma'am thank you," she replied.

The older lady motioned for her to take a seat at the table where Curtis was already nursing a strong cup of coffee. The smell was delicious. He appeared to be reading his Bible. He stopped momentarily and smiled warmly in her direction. His gold rimmed reading glasses were halfway down his nose.

"I fixed you a big breakfast and I hope you're hungry because we believe in eating around this house. Right dear?"

Helen gave her husband a wink.

"Amen," he replied patting his stomach and laughing. Addy wished she could enjoy this great breakfast without having to bring up anything negative but she knew she had to get it out of the way.

"Thank you both for everything you've done; helping me. You see, my mom's in the hospital dying and we just got the news she was brain dead last night."

Helen gasped and Curtis nodded as if this information was a revelation to him of why he found her about to dive into a frozen river.

165

"You poor child," Helen exclaimed. "I bet your father's worried sick about you."

"No ma'am. My dad passed away last year and my mom remarried but we aren't close. I really have nobody, but don't worry. I won't be a bother. I have aunts and uncles I can call."

Her story sounded so tragic that even she couldn't believe it really happened to her and not to someone in a movie.

"You know honey, God doesn't want you solving your problems like you tried to last night," Curtis reminded her. "He loves you and will be there for you even if you don't have anyone else in the whole world. He will never leave you or forsake you child."

He stared at her in a way that made her feel like he was reading her soul. She hung her head in shame and nodded that she understood.

"Yes sir. I know that now. I'm really sorry. I was just upset and scared," she lied, knowing there was so much more to it. She hadn't bothered to mention the baby or why her mother was dying. God must be mocking her by sending a preacher to stop her suicide. She could see the irony in it, for sure.

After breakfast, Helen presented her with the freshly laundered clothes she had been wearing the night before. The hole was still in the leg of her pants as a reminder of how her night almost ended. She changed, thanking Helen again for letting her stay the night. Curtis had offered to drive her home or to the hospital, whichever she chose. She tried to decline but he wouldn't take no for an answer. Addy chose to go home.

Chapter 35

Pastor Campbell was surprised to see where she lived. He was familiar with the elder Mr. Thomas, Bret's father. He was a good man. He and his wife had waited late in life to have a child but he recalled how they doted on the boy when he was small. Curtis was also shocked to find out that their son had married this girl's mother. The age difference must be substantial, he thought. Oh well, it wasn't for him to judge. He had definitely seen stranger couples in his lifetime.

Pulling the car in front of the house, he pushed the shifter into park and turned to Addy.

"Helen and I would love it if you would come visit us again; maybe even go to a service with us at our church. I preach a mean sermon," he added with a grin.

How could she tell him that God did not want her in his house? She had betrayed God by hurting her mother and trying to take her own life. She was pretty sure that God had a long list of reasons why she was one of his least favorite human beings.

"We would love to get to know you better Addy."

"Thank you. I would like that sir."

He smiled and asked if she would allow him to pray with her. She couldn't be rude and tell him no so she nodded in silent agreement. Curtis bowed his head and reached to clasp her hand.

"Dear God, holy Lord of Lords, we thank you for your many blessings. We thank you for new friendships, especially for the new friend you have given us in Addy. God we pray for your protection over her life. We ask you to touch her mother and the rest of her family as they deal with the hardships at hand. We ask all these favors in the holy name of Jesus. Amen."

Addy entered the house to find it empty. There didn't seem to be anyone at home, not even Margie. She went into the kitchen for something to drink and while she was retrieving a glass from the cupboard, she heard the front door close. Voices. She could hear unfamiliar voices coming from the foyer. Curious, she sat down her glass and headed in that direction.

Bret was hanging his coat in the entryway closet. He had a much older man and woman with him. She recognized the couple from their pictures. This was Bret's mother and father who lived in Florida. Bret was visibly surprised to see her standing there watching them.

His parents had flown up from the sunshine state after he called to give them the awful news about Joanie. His mother had insisted that he needed his family close to him during this tragedy.

"Addy, I didn't know you were home. This is my mom and dad. Harold and Muriel Thomas. They came up to be with us through this terrible situation with your mom."

Harold was the first to offer his hand in greeting.

"It's nice to meet you Addy. We're so sorry about your mother," he added sincerely. Muriel stepped

168

forward and threw her arms around Addy in a sympathetic hug.

"Yes dear, we are so very sorry. Please feel free to consider us your family. We're here for you and Bret."

How could she dislike these folks? She couldn't. They were genuine and she liked that. She couldn't help thinking that if her mother were awake their visit would not be such a polite one. She had the feeling that Joanie was not their kind of person. These people were well off but didn't make any effort to put on airs.

"Thank you ma'am. That means a lot," she replied.

She didn't want to be rude but she had things she needed to do and there was an urgency she couldn't ignore. She turned her attention to Bret.

"Where's Margie?"

"Margie's our cook," he explained to his parents. "I gave her the day off," he answered.

This was the information she needed. Margie wasn't here so she would go to her.

"I hope you both will excuse me. I've got somewhere important I need to be. I hope to see you both later on."

Addy was going to see Margie for a reason. She needed someone she trusted to know the truth. She needed counsel. Margie was the closest thing to a parent she had left. She knew it probably looked heartless that she didn't ask Bret for an update on her mother's condition. She couldn't help that. It would have to wait. This could not.

Her plan was to change into a different outfit because looking at the rip in her pants reminded her of being glued to the side of a freezing cold metal railing. Once she had showered and changed she called a taxi to take her down to the hospital where she could pick up her car and head over to Margie's house.

Feeling somewhat better after showering, Addy decided to wait downstairs for the taxi to arrive. Pulling her handbag over her shoulder she headed down to the foyer. Walking towards the sitting room entrance she could hear Bret and his father carrying on what could only be described as a hushed conversation. She heard her mom's name mentioned and suddenly it made her angry. Why were they discussing Joanie in hushed tones; behind her back?

The closer she got, the clearer the conversation became. Stopping just short of the entryway she heard Harold scolding his son.

"Son, I tried to tell you what you were getting into and you refused to listen to me."

"Dad, don't start this. You know there is no way I could have predicted this," Bret whined defensively. She could hear his father's tone change to condescending.

"You couldn't have predicted what Bret? You couldn't have predicted that screwing around with a married older woman would have consequences? You destroyed that man's marriage, stole his wife and knocked up his daughter. What's wrong with you son? You weren't raised to think this whole mess is acceptable," Harold ranted.

What was this man saying? Bret had not even met her mother until after her father had died. Had he?

"Dad, why do you always have to make me feel stupid? She was great when we met. Yes, she was married but he took advantage of her. He was cruel to her. She told me he even smacked her around. She didn't deserve that Dad. I wanted to give her a better life."

Harold chuckled and said, "If you fell for that story son, the college education I paid for was all for nothing." He was raking Bret over the coals for falling prey to Joanie's obvious lies.

Addy couldn't believe her ears. Her mother had cheated on her father. Her mother had knowingly betrayed their family and to make matters worse, she had let her boyfriend believe she had been an abused wife.

She was disgusted to her core. For the first time since Joanie's accident, Addy was glad it happened. She hoped her mother would burn in Hell when it was her time to go. She felt a hate burning inside of her stomach that threatened to consume her. Bret knew about it and he lied. He had betrayed her as badly as her mother. Now, he had told his father about the baby.

She wanted to kill him. She wanted Bret to know the loss, pain and grief that she had known when he destroyed her family. She wanted him to pay. Dropping her handbag onto the floor, she stepped just inside the sitting room doorway. The loud smacking sound of her bag hitting the floor made both men look her way.

"You despicable scumbag!" she screamed.

Looking confused, Bret tried to walk her way.

"Don't come near me! You stole my family. You took my mom away from my dad and you lied for her. I trusted you! I trusted you and you betrayed me. I hate you," she screamed louder with every sentence.

Harold simply stood back and watched his son face his accuser. He knew he could offer no defense for Bret. The very thing he had pleaded with his son not to do was coming full circle to ruin him now.

"Addy, please listen to me," he begged. The urge to slap him across the face was overpowering.

Suddenly a sharp pain shot across her lower abdomen. The pain was so strong that it caused her to cry out and clutch her stomach. It wasn't letting up, only getting stronger every second. She felt as if someone or something were splitting her in two across the middle. Running to her, Bret tried to reach out but she slapped his hands away.

"Addy, what's going on? Are you okay?"

"Get...away," she gasped through grunts and groans.

This made no sense. Where was this pain coming from? What was wrong with her? It felt hot and sharp and reached from one side of her all the way around to the

171

other side. It was becoming too difficult to stand and she was sinking down onto her knees.

In the background she could hear Harold calling 9-1-1. He was telling the operator she was pregnant. On her knees, bent forward she was crying in agony when she noticed the blood. It had soaked through her pants and had begun to pool onto the floor under her.

The ambulance finally arrived. She could hear them running into the foyer in her direction. Voices were coming at her from all directions. A female EMT had bent over Addy and was trying to calm her down. She wanted to stop crying but the pain was so intense she could hardly catch her breath. The blood, she could smell it. It was pungent, hot and sticky; and it was still coming.

She could hear the urgency in the voices of the medical workers. Something was terribly wrong. She knew it. Was it the baby? Was it something else? One of the male EMTs compassionately asked her to open her mouth and allow him to place something on her tongue to dissolve. She managed to do as he asked and within seconds her eyelids were very heavy. She couldn't hold them open any longer. As darkness enfolded her, she could feel them wheeling her out of the room.

Chapter 36

Waking up to find herself in a hospital was becoming an unpleasant habit these days. She felt so drowsy and groggy. What had they given her? Addy remembered why she was here but she wasn't sure what had happened between bleeding on the floor and waking up.

The door to her room slowly cracked open and a nurse came through with Margie on her heels. Margie stood back near the window to give the nurse room to do her job. Addy was so very glad to see Margie.

"Good, you're awake," the nurse said. She had her chart in her hand and after checking the readout on all her machines, she wrote the information down.

"Can you tell me what happened to me? Do you know yet?"

The nurse, whose name tag read Barbara Dills, placed her hand on Addy's shoulder in a motherly fashion.

"I'm sorry but it seems that you have miscarried your pregnancy at six weeks. The doctor who checked you out when you arrived did a thorough list of tests and didn't find anything that would indicate the cause. It was ruled spontaneous. Stress, dehydration, over exertion--they can all be causes as well. You will still need to follow up with your personal doctor just to make sure there are no future issues overlooked. We're working on your discharge papers now and hopefully we will have you out of here soon."

Patting her shoulder lightly she added, "I'm so sorry for your loss honey." Nurse Dills waited a moment as if expecting Addy to have more questions.

"Thank you," was the only reply Addy could muster.

Once the nurse had excused herself and left the room, Margie came over to the bedside and hugged Addy.

"Oh dear, I'm so sorry about the baby. Do you need me to call Drew? Is there anything I can do for you?"

Margie was indeed one of the best people she ever knew. She was there for her when her own mother had turned her back. This woman was no blood relation to her and owed her nothing but yet she had shown her more love in the months they had known one another than most people experience in a lifetime. She wanted to repay her somehow and the only way that came to mind was honesty. She wanted to be completely truthful with Margie.

Addy started at the beginning. She told Margie about her mom marrying Bret after her father's death. She told her about the change in Joanie, the friendship she forged with Bret and that fateful birthday when that friendship went too far. She even shared the truth about the day her mother had the accident and how Drew found out about the baby. Addy didn't fail to include her attempted suicide and how she found out the depth of her mother's deception which, she believed, ultimately led her to her current situation.

When she had finished her story, Margie was crying so hard she had to pull a tissue out of her purse to blow her nose.

"You probably see me for the awful person I am now but I figured I owed you the truth. You've been too good to me to keep lying to you."

Margie dabbed her nose with her tissue and spoke with gentle yet firm authority.

"Listen up child. You need to know that nothing you could ever do would make me not love you anymore and thinking God doesn't love you anymore is ridiculous! Wipe that thought out of your head right now. I'm just grateful to whoever the people were that saved you from hurting yourself."

Addy sighed loudly and said, "Yes, they are good people. Helen and Curtis Campbell are their names. They preach at Dunlevy Baptist in Bramwell." Margie's eyes lit up.

"Well my goodness. The Lord truly does work in mysterious ways. Helen is a good friend of mine. We don't get to see each other as often as we'd like these days but we still find time to talk on the phone regularly."

What a small world. Addy could easily see these two women as friends. She bet that when the two of them got together, they were a handful. She looked over at Margie and all at once a wave of complete and utter sadness swept over her and she began to cry.

"Oh don't cry honey," Margie soothed. "You just sit tight and I'll be right back. I promise." She jumped up and was out the door in a flash.

Almost a half hour had passed before she returned. Addy had begun to worry that Margie wouldn't be back; that she had given up on her and chose to leave her all alone. Her stomach still hurt. Whatever they had given her for pain was beginning to wear off. It wasn't as bad as before but there was a lot of pressure. It felt strange to know that when she woke up this morning she had another human life growing inside of her and now, just like that, it was gone.

When Margie returned, she wasn't alone. Helen Campbell was with her. Instead of looking on her with pity, Helen smiled and said, "Long time no see." It was a joke at such an inopportune time but it made Addy laugh. She was glad because she didn't want anyone's pity. She only wanted someone to help her see where to go from here.

The three ladies had a long talk while waiting for Addy to be released. Margie had told Helen the whole story on the way over. Neither woman had judged her or even scolded her. Not once had they told her she should have known better. They had only shown her love and acceptance. They had also offered her something else; something far more special. They offered her a chance at a new life. Helen had asked Addy to come stay with them and finish high school in their district. The old Addy wouldn't have accepted such an offer from a virtual stranger but the new Addy jumped at the chance.

The hospital finally discharged her with a long list of dos and don'ts as well as strict orders to rest and follow up with Dr. Taylor in a week. The two women helped her to the car and drove directly to Bret's house. The plan was in place and each of them knew their part. They entered the house and proceeded straight to Addy's set of rooms upstairs. They began filling bags with clothing and personal items when Bret walked in.

"What's going on here? Why are you packing? Someone answer me!" he yelled.

"Addy will be coming to stay with us," Helen replied while collecting the things on the nightstand.

"Who are you?" Bret asked. "Addy isn't going anywhere carrying my child!"

He had thrown this information out there as if he were spilling the beans to the whole world. She could tell by the look on his face that he thought this fact gave him the final word. Addy was not about to let him have his moment of superiority, even if it killed her. She stood her ground and faced him.

"First of all, *she* is the person who convinced me that my life was worth living. Second, there is no baby. Thanks to your lies and schemes I lost the baby when I bled all over your floor. Now, you *will* let me go or I may remember our encounter on the sofa very differently to the police. Then who is going to believe anything you say, especially your crazy story about my mom's accident? You just try and stop me Bret and you will see what happens," she warned.

He could see the steely reserve in her eyes. She was dead serious. She would be leaving his house and there was nothing he could do about it.

"Son, let her go. Now," Harold ordered from the doorway. He shifted his gaze to Addy and said, "Young lady, I do not appreciate you threatening my son in his own home. It is unfortunate what happened to the baby and we are willing to compensate you for your loss but I believe we all agree that it's time for you to move on."

"Dad, she can't leave!" Bret shouted.

"Bret, shut your mouth," his father snapped.

"Thank you sir, but there is no *compensation* for what I've lost," she responded. The women were carrying bags out the door.

"Wait, you're just going to leave with your mom like she is?" Bret asked incredulously. Addy stopped walking but never turned to face him.

"She left me long ago. She's your wife now."

Helen and Margie helped her into the car after they loaded her bags into the trunk.

"You okay dear?"

"Yes, Miss Helen. I'm better than I've been in a long time."

As they drove away from the house, Addy refused to look back. She never wanted to look back again.

177

Epilogue

Addy spent the next few weeks recovering. Living with Helen and Curtis was helping to heal a wound that had been open and raw for far too long. They were wonderful people who not only lived by example but who mirrored the true love of God.

They had prayed with her and helped her see that Jesus still loved her. She knew now that He had seen her future mistakes as he hung on the cross; he still chose to die for her sins. He gave his life to make her wrongs right and she loved him for it.

Addy accepted God's forgiveness and gave her life back to Christ. She became a regular attender of Dunlevy Baptist Church and everyone welcomed her like family.

Three weeks into her stay with the Campbells, Margie dropped by one day like she normally did but this time she had news. Bret had made the decision to turn off the machines that had been keeping Joanie alive. The funeral would be scheduled for the following Monday. Addy's family would all be attending and many of them had asked where she could be found. Anticipating this happening, Addy had left strict instructions not to give her information out to anyone in her family.

Margie had respected her wishes and simply denied knowledge of her whereabouts. Bret told the family he thought she had gotten a job in another town and transferred schools. The family found it odd but since most of them were unaware of what the past year and a half had been like for them, they didn't question it.

Addy didn't go to the funeral to mourn her mother. That was something she had spent plenty of time doing while Joanie still lived. Death was behind her now and she wanted only to concentrate on her future.

Once her doctor released her to go back to school, she changed high schools and worked her tail off trying to catch up on everything she missed while recuperating. She stayed to herself mostly and studied a lot. She was never unfriendly but most students were kept at arm's length, never allowed to get too close. This was how she treated most people except for her blessed benefactors and her church family. She volunteered constantly for anything the church needed. She had even begun counseling teen girls who needed help or just had no one else to confide in. God had taken the bad in her life and used it to help others. She felt so privileged to be able to use her misfortune for good.

The following spring was her high school graduation and she was excited. Plans were already in the works for her to attend community college where she would work towards a degree in sociology as well as psychology. Her goal was to counsel runaways.

Curtis and Helen were so proud of her. In the fifteen months she had been in their lives, she had become the daughter they never had. Her presence had filled their home with life and love like they never imagined. God had blessed them with an amazing gift that cold night on Flaggers Bridge. A gift they would be grateful for every day of their lives.

Addy assembled with the rest of her graduating class and one by one they lined up in their caps and gowns to walk past the many onlookers. She gazed across the sea of faces and thought of her father. He would be so proud of her today. She could imagine him clapping and whistling as she walked by. The image gave her comfort. She briefly thought of her mother and the baby she never knew. A pang of sadness gripped her heart, but only for a moment because in the midst of the huge crowd she saw Curtis and Helen sitting next to Margie and her family. The look of happiness and pride on their faces made up for it all. She offered up a silent prayer of thanks as the graduation procession walked down the field and took their seats. Brushing a tear off her face she remembered a favorite Bible verse and smiled.

"But one thing I do: forgetting what lies behind and straining forward to what lies ahead." (Phillippians 3:13)